Sta uture.

HOOK

Hook must sink into obscurity to escape the vengeance of the Boosted Men searching him out among the stars. He finds such a place of security in Star City.

Orbiting a relatively primitive planet, Star City is a mighty complex housing many thousands of humanoids devoted entirely to the pursuit of pleasure. Hook enjoys many pleasant days there.

Gradually it punctures his consciousness that all is not as friendly and gentle as it appears, and that pleasure seems eternally to be based on someone else's pain.

Also in this series and available from NEL:

HOOK 1: WHIRLPOOL OF STARS
HOOK 2: THE BOOSTED MAN

Star City

NEW ENGLISH LIBRARY
TIMES MIRROR

For
SIMON RACK
and the Chronicler of his adventures,
Laurence James.

An NEL Original

*

FIRST NEL PAPERBACK EDITION OCTOBER 1974

*

NEL Books are published by The New English Library Limited from Barnard's Inn, Holborn, London E.C.1. Made and printed in Great Britain by C. Nicholls & Company Ltd

45001963 2

CHAPTER ONE

"WE'LL slit this Hook's throat," said Walton Gaines, with all the dark authority in his voice reaching clearly from the galley to where Hook sat at the controls of the space cutter. "And slip him into space a day out from Stellopolis."

"We can beam in a fresh pilot from there," said Locum Hauser, his voice incisive against the metalloy hull.

"Getting rid of Hook will be a pleasure." Happy Derning's voice rolled comfortably, with a chuckle, from where he sat drinking coffee in the galley. The other member of the quartet, Cher-charon, had no need to speak to make his feelings known.

Hook detested inefficiency in others and hated it wholeheartedly in himself. Mistakes spawned from inefficiency. Hook had made many mistakes in his time – perhaps the chief of which was being born into the hundred and first century at all, although to blame himself for that smacked of vulgar ostentation – and he knew with a galactic adventurer's vulnerable philosophy that he would make many more. That was, he conceded, if he survived his last mistake which had been to join up with this unlovely foursome. Now they thought the job for which they had sought his aid was over they planned to kill him off.

In that they merely joined a long line of infinitely more powerful forces which had attempted to kill off Ryder Hook. You had to feel sorry for them, really.

These four fools planning their petty deviltry had no idea, of course, that Hook was able to overhear them and all their plans quite clearly. They laboured under the misapprehension that he was just another ruffian and criminal of the galaxy, like themselves, living on his wits and ready to turn a dishonest pek no matter who suffered along the way. His mistake had been teaming up with them in the first place. But the proposition had sounded attractive. A simple matter of stealing this space cutter, loading her with fifty kilos of art – micro-recordings of a thousand stellar system's cultural heritages, all stolen from Bandong's central archives – and taking her across a mere twenty parsecs or so to Stellopolis and there disposing of the cargo with profit all round. The theft angle had pleased Hook most, for Bandong had fallen into the hands of the Boosted Men, and he'd extricated himself with some difficulty, so that the removal of the archival material duplicates had come as something of a bonus.

As far as Ryder Hook was concerned, a Boosted Man spelled bad news wherever he might be encountered.

And yet – and yet that evil craving for the powers the proximity of a Boosted Man conferred on Ryder Hook obsessed him with hungers he knew with fifty percent of his senses he must fight until death, and the remaining fifty percent he was helpless to resist, for the sheer lure and marvel of becoming even for a short time surrogate Boosted Man drugged him in ways unknown to other mortals. To hell with all the Novamen! He was just Ryder Hook, outcast and wayfarer of the galaxy, without a wrist credit card, member of no economic conglomerate or multi-system organisation, member of no union, owing allegiance to no single planet or system or armed service. He was Ryder Hook. He stood alone in the whirlpool of stars.

These four star-rats, now, all belonged to an econorg, all boasted a wrist credit card.

In that, they felt themselves to be far superior to a loner, immeasurably above an outcast of the galaxy who lacked any form of protection from his parent organisation.

"You going to do it yourself, Walt, or c'n I –?"

"I think, Happy, this is more Locum's style."

"Maybe, but I'd enjoy it!"

"Let me handle it, Happy," said Locum Hauser, cool, hard, a professional killer. "You'd bust a gut laughing and forget to slit his throat."

"I've cut throats in my time!"

"All right," said Walton Gaines, over-riding them. "Locum does it. We get Hook talking, and then –"

"A nice clean job."

Hook considered.

These four could as easily have simply tossed him out through the air lock. But they kept harping on slitting his throat. No doubt they liked the sight of blood. There were people like that in the galaxy.

Hook pulled back the cuff of his left sleeve. He wore his familiar indifferent-blue tunic and trousers, and his famous old black boots rested four square on the control throne's pedestal, ready to kick instantly at any of the foot-operated control devices, so situated for attention when his hands were fully occupied. The plain indifferent-blue of the tunic, without any red streaks over shoulders and outside arms was necessary. When he had to he wore what he had to; as a rule he liked to wear indiscriminate, off-putting, unidentifiable clothes. That way he could blend with a multitude of backgrounds.

On his left wrist the nasty little Delling had been mounted, coupled in with his muscle and nervous system, so that a twitch of muscles of the right intensity would bring the dis-gel gun instantly into action. Most people – all normal people – wore the tiny hideaway guns on their right wrists. Their left wrists held the sealed credit cards. Hook had, before now, found some amusement and profit from that left-handed gun.

So. He could simply walk back to the galley and melt the four men down into pools of jelly. They could never match him for speed, even in his normal and un-Boosted state. He half rose, the decision firm and dominant in his brain.

The moral philosophy was all old and worked-out and with cobwebs festooning the neat conclusions.

If a man tried to kill Ryder Hook that man went in peril of his own life. Hook knew he had no more right to life than any other man; but that meant that a killer had no more right to life than did Ryder Hook. So if one was to die, Hook felt it preferable it should not be Ryder Hook. He might be odd or peculiar in that life-long belief; but that was the way he was.

He paused.

Mortality. Killing. States of being and states of unconsciousness. Violence. Well, he'd had his share of that. But he paused, and then sat down again. The space cutter sped between the stars on course, predicted to planetfall, aimed and routed and perfectly functioning in every department. Hook both loved and hated space. He liked watching the stars and the lazy drift of the spiral arms and the weird shapes made by clouds of dust so thin they could be seen only in light-year condensations. He felt at times that a galactic roamer had the best of all worlds. At other times he knew he was an outcast, and then he would metaphorically shake his fist at the damned stars and bawl at them to go to hell. Now he faced a problem that should be so easily settled he would think no more of it than buying a good algae-steak dinner.

Four men had gone into partnership with him. Now they had successfully pulled off the coup these four wished to dispose of him so as to deny him his share of the proceeds. The money metal would mean to Hook only a little extra time to push back the barrier when he must again do something about making a living. He could kill them before they killed him. That was not unknown.

But Hook liked the elegant solution to a problem.

Often the most elegant way of dealing with trouble was to shoot first. Hook knew that. But, here and now, there was another way that amused him.

Deliberately he checked the controls. The space cutter was just that, a tiny craft with a minimum of luxury and with engines that would fling her across space at ftl rates high in the measurements of starship velocities. Without the refinements of a space yacht and yet with all the power necessary for interstellar travel she was a far cry from a simple interplanetary vessel. She was, in short, valuable property.

Hook knew her control system, knew her engines, knew her foibles. Her onboard computer housed low in her belly gave output terminals on the flank of the control room, and here Hook checked one final time. The cutter – her name was

Spokane – remained firmly on course for Stellopolis. Once there she would not need to go into a parking orbit around the city unless there was a delay at the landing facility. She could barrel straight in, check herself out, using whatever identification Hook, as the pilot, might think fit, and so berth. The four of them, Walton Gaines, Happy Derning, Locum Hauser and Cher-charon, had been glad to have a fully-qualified space pilot, checked out on interstellar vessels of this tonnage, join them, for none could pilot a spaceship. The art and science was confined, as of necessity it must be, to those few who lasted the strenuous course required. They thought Hook was a spaceman who had, for one reason or another, been beached. Without him they could never have done what they had done. But now they were near enough Stellopolis to plan murder, they felt confident they could beam up a new pilot on the transmat and replace Ryder Hook.

Replacing Ryder Hook in this man's galaxy was a task beyond them, and certainly beyond most mortals.

Those famous old black boots of Ryder Hook's held many intriguing instruments for performing many unpleasant catastrophes upon machinery; but it was scarcely necessary for him to employ that arsenal of mayhem now. A few simple passes over the controls, setting up a pattern of mutual incompatibility, a cross-check to ensure that he had not overdone the amusement and thus precipitated total catastrophe, and he could sit back and look with a sombre joy upon the release button.

An elegant solution. He could easily have yanked out his Tonota Eighty and blasted a dirty great hole in the guidance systems, fouled up the ship's neural synapses, made a slagged and smoking heap of the controls; this way held that priceless gift of inner amusement that came so high in this hard and merciless galaxy.

"I'm going to catch some sleep-time now," came Gaines' voice from the galley, mingled with the sounds of men rising and cups being replaced. "First thing tomorrow ship-time. Check?"

"All IQ, Walton," said Locum Hauser. Hook could quite plainly hear the sibilant satisfaction in that smooth voice. Incisive, hard, smooth and deadly, that was Locum Hauser, and for all that Walton Gaines, who was a Homo sapiens, counted himself as the leader of the quartette, Locum Hauser, the mal, held a real and terrifying power.

Hook listened with ears more finely tuned than any Homo sapiens had a right to own. They were a part of the heritage of his RCI. processing that had given him his extraordinary body. His hand hovered over the release button on the board.

Might it not be even more amusing to let these four petty-minded little killers spend one more night luxuriating in the cleverness of their scheme? Then Ryder Hook's sound commonsense asserted itself. Hauser might become impatient. That clown Happy Derning, who was a Noruba from out past Commercesh way, might decide he wanted the fun of slashing Hook's throat first, and to hell with Gaines and Hauser. No, Hook decided, he had to let these men know the state of the game right now.

He flicked the release button.

Smoke began to pour out of cracks in the control board, and the maze of green lights shining from the control console abruptly became measle-speckled with reds. Measles, like most diseases, was a mere racial memory, a footnote in the history books. But it fitted that board. Hook chuckled.

"Hey!" he shouted, backing off from the throne. The ship was perfectly IQ he'd made sure of that. "Hey!"

They came arunning – or, in the case of Cher-charon – a-wriggling.

"What the hell's going on here –" bellowed Gaines, his high colour even more scarlet and his eyes enraged as he saw the smoke and smelled the charred insulation fumes.

"Automatics overloaded," said Hook. He pushed past Gaines and snatched down the zer-dumper. The red cylinder yielded to his first press and began to squirt flame-suppressant. "Don't just stand there! Get with it."

Happy Derning goggled, his mal face vicious, his fingers twisting and twirling one tubular ear.

"The automatics, did you say, you stupid –" began Hauser. Then he recollected himself. "How did it happen?"

Hook did not smile, that was not his style; but he cocked

an evil eye at Hauser. "If you knew anything about astrogation or handling a spaceship you'd have no need to ask such a damn fool question. This bucket needs servicing. I told you that back at Bandong. But you wouldn't listen."

"You said you could fly her to Stellopolis –"

"So I can. But I'll have to pilot her in all the way now. There's a magnetic anomaly storm brewing up dead on course. Without the autos I'll have to barrel her through on manuals – you're lucky I know how."

For a moment he wondered if he'd overplayed his hand.

Well, if he had and they were foolish enough to go ahead with their plan, the Delling snugged against his wrist, and he would back himself to dis-gel the four of them before the first cleared his own wrist gun.

Gaines said: "When we're within range of Stellopolis – can you match velocities with the city?"

Almost, then, Ryder Hook became tired of this farce.

Almost, he blasted these four fools where they stood.

The elegance of his own plan now seemed to him mere posturing. These four were vermin of the spaceways and therefore would not be missed. But he'd had some vague and holy-joe idea that he ought to spare their lives because killing was an evil thing. So it was. But if they persisted in foolishness . . .

Not a patient man when it came to idiots, Ryder Hook had had long experience in schooling himself to suffer fools. He needed all that patience so hardly-learned in those moments as the four criminals slowly forced themselves to accept the fact that if they wanted to reach star city alive only Ryder Hook could take them there.

How Ed Malcom would have smiled in his quiet warm way to see Hook now. Almost, then, Hook wanted to turn back in his memory and say: "See, Ed, what sweetness and light lets a man in for?" But Ed had the right answers; sometimes Hook felt a sad uneasiness that he was not built of the stern stuff from which martyrs are fabricated.

The space cutter *Spokane* sped through the dusty emptiness of space and Hook's four associates composed themselves for sleep. This ship night had been programme-alarmed to last seven hours terrestrial, and sharp on the following ship morning the four rolled out, yawning, knuckling their eyes, reaching for the a.m. pep-tab. Hook had dozed on and off during the night when the lights turned down and his capacity for being awakened if a fly buzzed too close or an unfriendly footfall disturbed the air had not been called into operation.

"We make Stellopolis today, then," said Happy Derning, making conversation, as always laughing. For a mal he might have made a halfway decent human being, considered Hook with some sour bias, had the man not taken up with criminal associates. Happy usually had a fatuous smile curving his lips, and, like a number of people Hook knew – including himself when circumstances demanded – he could chuckle with the best. A man who could chuckle at life wasn't all bad. At least, there was some hope for him, as there could be precious little for the man who frowned on chuckling as beneath his dignity.

"Ever been to this star city before?" Walton Gaines was fully in command of the situation again, as he saw it. His high colour positively glowed over the breakfast table.

No-one had. Hook had travelled a great deal of the galaxy; but no man was going to see every sun and every planet in even the long lifetimes granted to people in the hundred and first century.

"It's a fabulous place." Gaines waxed lyrical, and Hook had to take a sip of his morning tea to hide his smile. Like any civilised man, Hook drank tea whenever he could. The idea of coffee for breakfast was bad enough; the conception that some people drank coffee as their first drink of the day nauseated him.

"Plenty of girls there?"

Gaines glanced across at Locum Hauser.

"All you can desire, Locum. Pleasure is an art on Stellopolis. Something to do with their religion – or maybe their politics. It don't matter which. When we sell this lot we'll have money metal to back our credit cards."

"Come the day," said Happy Derning.

Credit cards were fine – essential unless you were as rough, tough and ruthless a person as, for instance, was Ryder Hook – but they had still to be backed with a credit balance with the bank of your econorg. No balance, no credit; no credit, no protection. No protection; welcome to the Ryder Hook fanclub, all dues unpaid.

"We'd never have made it without you, Hook." Gaines lowered his cup and stared at Hook. "What you plan to do?"

Hook knew he meant after they had unloaded the fifty kilos of art micro-recordings.

"Ship out, I think."

"Stellopolis can offer a man a great deal. Me, I'm going to have myself a good time before I move on."

"Me, too," said Happy Derning, rolling his ear tube with great and anticipatory wallowings of pleasure.

Locum Hauser, darkly brooding as usual, said nothing. But the way he sliced his algae-ham steak told Hook all he needed to know of the man's thought processes.

Cher-charon, of course, remained silent. He wriggled his sinuous length more comfortably around the stainless steel perch-bar he occupied for meals and sucked delicately through one of his facial tubes. He was drinking orange juice, an affectation of the galaxy-weary travellers of his home system of Sanzaire. The Sanzaireans were carnivorous; meat eating snake-like people of immense subtlety and dissimulation they aped the ways of others to show that although they were a race recently introduced to the galactic scene they were fully aware and fully deserving of interstellar status. For a carnivore to drink orange juice was a refinement that left Hook, for one, experiencing a mockery he would not put into words on the offchance the affectation might become a racial trait. Hook let other people mind their own business if it did not interfere with his own.

Now Cher-charon wiggled a tendril or two and the others accepted this mute signal as an indication he would decide later. When the Sanzairean wished to converse with a member of a race whose communications were carried by sound waves he had to couple in the transceiver strapped somewhere to his sinuous body and let the transducers interpret emotions and states of feeling and motives into coded language sections.

Gaines stood up with his habitual air of decision. The two

mals and Cher-charon looked up at him. Hook, also, looked up.

"We berth today. You, Hook, had better have the cover story word perfect. We don't want trouble with the port authority. You two be ready to break out the cargo. You, Cher, keep out anybody who tries to sniff around."

A needle-barb appeared and disappeared from one of the Sanzairean's tendrils. That was his way of saying he accepted the order and understood it.

The two mals rolled their ear tubes, and Hauser said: "We c'n do that, Gaines. But you'd better check Hook's story."

Hook said: "We're space cutter *Fantom.* Inbound from Sparkholm Eleven. Traders. No trouble. From what Gaines says of Stellopolis they'll welcome us with open arms."

Cher-charon flipped a tendril at this, a habitual response. What his transceiver had translated Hook's word into for his own comprehension might never be known by a human who had no cortico processes to parallel what went on in the Sanzairean's brain.

"All the same, I'll be there when we get the port authority call."

Gaines did as he had promised; but, as Hook had promised, the port authority of this star city made no trouble at all and were only too anxious to clear away the formalities as quickly as possible so that the enticing items quickly listed on the flash-out panel could be inspected. For a people living for pleasure the arrival of this kind of merchandise spelled excitement. In this Hook was quite right; he was to discover that other excitements existed that could not be so easily quantified. The space cutter swooped into the indicated entry port of the star city. Hook took her in with a quiet sobriety he knew would not attract unwelcome attention. He saw the way the four of them were twitching as they waited for the next second to bring a challenge, the statement "You are space cutter *Spokane,* stolen from Bandong. You are under arrest."

No challenge blared at them from the speaker.

"We're in, by Verthash!" said Happy Derning, delighted.

The damage Hook had done to the controls of the cutter

had been finely selected, and the over-ride he had had to by-pass which would have automatically closeted off the danger area could still function with what he had left. He swept his hands across the board, shutting it down. That eternal thrilling subcutaneous trilling of the cutter's engine died. With a final shudder and tremble that unheard noise vanished.

"We're in!" said Walton Gaines, as though he had done it all.

Hook started to stand up. He rose from the pilot's throne.

A shape, a shadow, a fleeting movement.

He knew, in that flashing instant of time, he understood that he had made a mistake with these men, and now he had compounded that mistake. Forced to allow him to live whilst he brought them into Stellopolis safely, now they were here they had no further use for him. Fifty kilos of micro-recorded art sounded better to them split four ways than split five.

And they were old comrades in the criminal way of life.

Hook saw the steel bar slicing down towards his head.

He saw that maniacal glare in Locum Hauser's dark eyes.

The steel bar smashed into his skull.

CHAPTER TWO

THE steel bar bounced.

For any normal man that steel bar powered by all the dark ferocity of a homicidal maniac would have shattered his skull into bloody fragments. Blood and brains would have spurted past the splintered bones. But, then, Ryder Hook was not a normal man. He was not a superman. He had to tell himself that again and again, and – as now – he had to remind himself that he was merely an ordinary man to whom the machinations of RCI had given extraordinary powers.

Hook reared up, snatched the bar from the abruptly nerveless fingers of Locum Hauser. The mal glared at Hook as though confronted with all the foul devils of his own mythologies made manifest in the flesh of the Earthman.

"You gonil!" screamed Hauser. Hook saw with absolute clarity the way the mal's muscles tensed for the instantaneous drawing of the nasty little dis-gel gun tucked up his sleeve. With muscles that, although not in Boosted condition, were far more powerful, far faster, far more subtle than anyone had any right to expect, Hook continued with the swing of the bar. He swung it down and around and up and the end took Hauser's hand from beneath and smashed it upwards. The dis-gel discharge splattered the overhead, and both Homo sapiens and mal moved instinctively aside so as not to be spattered by so much as a single drop.

Only then, and not before, did Hook bother to hit the mal.

Hauser went down.

A voice lifted from the cabin area abaft the pilot's compartment.

"Hurry up, Locum! The enforcers will be aboard soon."

Hook took out the Tonota Eighty. The gun was ridiculously big for onboard work, and if fired would take most of the hull plating away with it in the direction of its blast. But Hook wouldn't mind that. These three curds needed to be over-awed instantly. He stepped into the cabin.

A mal mouth and a Homo sapiens mouth dropped open, and a Sanzairean mouth tendril curled abruptly, like a sensitive frond of an Earthside fern.

Hook showed them the gun.

Not that they were likely to miss the thing; but Hook was a man who liked to copper-bottom his bets, a man who would never take a chance unless that chance represented the best course in the circumstances. Then, of course, he took insane risks that left other people shivering with awed fright.

"Tell me," Ryder Hook said to them. "Why I should not kill you now?"

Gaines and Derning gobbled out words at once, together, backing away, holding their hands palms outwards before them, shaking with a fear that had no power to move Ryder Hook.

Hook's eyes regarded them with that intense brown gaze that, so he had been told – surlily – seemed to drill through a man. He remained perfectly aware of The Sanzairean, Cher-charon, who wriggled into an S-shaped bend, his body undulating with beautiful symmetry. His tendrils were now all folded, his mouth tubes tucked out of the way.

At last Gaines managed to bellow louder than Happy Derning.

"What are you playing at, Hook? We didn't know Locum was going to try to kill you! He was on his own! You've no cause to shoot me!"

Hook didn't bother to sigh over the clumsiness of it. He didn't even bother to say: "How do you know what Hauser was up to in the control cabin – out of your sight?"

Instead he wheeled, moved back a pace, his Delling snapped into his left hand and fired.

Cher-charon's fluidly beautiful body snapped through the air, the sinuous S-shape straightening and lengthening into a bar of scaled flesh and blood and bone. The tendrils sprang in time with the leap. Had Hook remained where he was he would have been impaled by a dozen needle-barbs.

The Delling's discharge squirted dis-gel over the forward parts of Cher-charon.

Now the Sanzairean made a sound.

His transceiver bubbled and squawked – and Cher-charon screamed.

His body melted.

From his tendrilled foreparts with their needle barbs, past his mouth tubes, past his upper body and the whole sinuous length of him, the dis-gel ate its way. The alien deliquesced.

Around his thorax area where he kept his hearts and lungs the melting power of the jelly slowed, flowed around and on down. Cher-charon had plated his scales in that area with a solution of armour-metal, a similar mix to the dip given to armour-plate-fab clothes, and Hook guessed he'd had no time to refurbish the rest of his scales before they'd pulled their robbery on Bandong. No doubt Cher-charon had figured on completing the job here in Stellopolis.

All that remained of that long and beautiful body lay puddling on the deck. It oozed between a cracked plate. It slopped over a former and dripped down between the treads. A being had been melted into a pool of foul scum.

Hook said: "So now you know what to expect."

Man and mal, they goggled at him, the breath caught in their throats.

"You two. Take your trousers off."

A single admonitory wave of the Tonota sent them into a frantic series of quick-strip hoppings. The Delling had vanished again up Hook's sleeve.

From the control section forward a voice spoke. It was not Locum Hauser. Besides being able to hear when the mal moved himself, Hook also had a fair idea of how long a person would be unconscious after he had hit him.

The voice said: "This is Stellopolis P.A. Open up your airlock or don't you want to berth here? What's keeping you?"

Hook waved the gun at the two trouserless and sorry specimens before him.

"In that locker, the spare oxy-bottle one. That's right. Squeeze in."

He slammed the door on them. The catch thunked satisfactorily.

He put his mouth against the smooth surface.

"If you bang or make a noise I'll see what a Tonota will do to quieten you."

He took himself off to the control section and, stepping over Hauser, who lay breathing in a charmingly stertorous way, thumbed the airlock release.

He would have fifteen minutes, terrestrial.

Enough.

Like many planets and star cities of the galaxy, Stellopolis had streamlined its disembarkation procedures. The Customs Officials ran their instruments over the ship. Down between the treads the last of Cher-charon quietly flowed and melted away. Nothing was left of him by the time the quarantine check robot trundled past above. Had the customs people put a forensic sniffer into action, now, the story would have been different . . .

"Art recordings, you said?"

"That's right." Hook did what was necessary with his face to make the man think he was smiling at him. "Fifty kilos. Thereabouts. All high-quality material. Sparkholm Eleven are going through a censorship phase, when the bluenoses get through with their burnings and destructs they'll wind up with a planetary cluster without culture."

"It happens. But it's good fortune for us." The Port Authority man was just that, a man, a member of Homo sapiens. There clung to him an aura of effeminacy, an air of refined decadence contributed to by his clothes – long flowing draperies with gold lace and plastic inserts of various glow-colours that subtly changed as he moved – and by the pallor underlying the normal cheerful copper colour one might expect in a galaxy where interbreeding had gone on for so long. However much of a dilettante he might appear, filling in his work quota in the Port Authority, Hook did not miss the gun strapped to his waist.

The gun snugged in a plax holster and was strapped down.

Hook fancied it was a Krifarm, probably a model nineteen; but he wouldn't bet on it. He admitted to a fascination for weapons of all kinds; he never allowed that fascination to develop into an obsession. Knowledge of weapons was essential to a man without a wrist credit card.

In addition, and without a credible doubt, the P.A. man would have some form of dis-gel gun coupled into his muscular and neural circuits and hidden beneath the flowing sleeve.

That would be on his right wrist.

That immediately brought up the thought that Hook would have to go through the tiresome business of accustoming these people to the amazing fact that he did not own a credit card.

He caught that one by the tail at once.

"I'd like payment in money metal, if it's all the same to you. That is, if the cargo is up to your requirements. I'm not overly particular –"

"Please, Taynor Hook! We on Stellopolis are always in the market for cultural artefacts. We hold these things in high esteem. Please do not consider spacing out until you have given us every opportunity to strike a bargain."

This wasn't the way the sharp operatives of the business galaxy talked; but then, Stellopolis was cut off from the main galactic current. It held undeniable attractions for men like Gaines and his crew, attractions that had brought him here in the first place. Hook fancied that even if the people of Stellopolis had been alerted by a call from Bandong, and knew that fifty kilos of art micro-recordings had been stolen from there, they'd be too anxious to lay their hands on the loot to report its discovery.

Hook was quite happy to play it along that way.

Robots detached the cargo pod from the cutter and quickly thereafter samples of the merchandise were run through screening scanners. Hook broke open a bottle and the P.A. man who was called Inlander, quaffed a glass in his languid way as the initial reports came in.

Eleven minutes had passed.

Inlander smiled and swung back from the screen.

"Excellent, – dear Taynor Hook! Quite exquisite. Work we have heard of and have long desired to see. There will be no difficulty in selling this package to us. You will sell it all?"

"Of course, Taynor Inlander."

"Fine, fine. Then I suggest you accompany me to the P.A. office. Business details are so tiresome. But we can complete this deal swiftly." A hint of a frown marred that languid expression. "You are sure you wish money metal?"

"Money metal will be admirable."

"As you wish."

There would be some sizeable bills to cover fifty kilos of this high-class merchandise. It was more than likely that this star city ran its own credit system, and only meshed with the great interstellar combines when it had to. Mind you Hook felt a genuine distaste for talking about the glorious work of men's minds and hearts, all the culture and art and beauty of a hundred stellar systems, the wealth of wonder contributed by men and women out of a desire to achieve a scrap of beauty against the great dark, as mere merchandise. But once a work of art was on the market – it did perforce become merchandise, to be haggled over.

That was the way of the galaxy.

On fourteen minutes Inlander, smiling, ushered Hook out of the space cutter and down the ramp leading onto the metalloy-hard decking the berthing area. Hook followed along, and found his right hand trailing quite naturally close to his holstered gun butt. Inlander chattered on, and Hook took a long look at the reception area. He'd visited star cities before and had found they came in all sizes and varieties. Stellopolis, judging from what he saw, was a fair-sized representative of the breed. From space the construction gave the random appearance of a gigantic collection of old boxes and domes and towers and linking ways with no centric thought to appearance. From time to time sections of the city might be detached to go about their own purposes, and sometimes another star city might happen by and the two join up to their mutual advantage. Indeed Stellopolis rivalled many a planetary city in extent, and in addition the three-dimensional aspect of the place gave a cubic capacity far beyond a normal planetary city, even those who towered miles into the air. Hook had no intention of hanging about here, for he would deal with Gaines and what was left of his criminal crew and then space out. But, in the unwelcome event he was forced to spend time here in star city he knew he could keep out of sight and remain undiscovered for as long as it might take – or so he read the signs.

He heard the chatter of annunciators heralding the arrival of starships as he passed through the glassite corridors of the Port Authority. There would be many berthing ports of this nature all around the irregular periphery of star city. Ships moved in and out constantly.

"Yes, Taynor Hook, we keep busy," said Inlander, ushering him into a palatial office with window-pics of exotic recorded animated views of planets star city had visited in its long travels among the stars. At the moment the city circled in orbit around a planet called Voyden, a world circling a nice gentle G-type star called Purlon Major. That sunshine flooded in through ports and windows, controlled and directed, mellow and pleasing. There might be inhabitants of the planet and no doubt the people of star city had set up the usual business arrangements with them. Many planets welcomed the arrival of a star city in orbit about them; others objected. It all depended on the psychological makeup of the parties concerned.

"I'd like to space out as soon as possible," said Hook.

"Of course – if you wish. But, my dear Taynor Hook, we Curlmen are proud of our city and can offer tremendous pleasures. We believe in luxury as a right of all men. And –" Here he laughed very pleasantly, displaying white teeth in what was for him a grandiose gesture. "– and we see to it that our life here is made as comfortable and luxurious as human ingenuity can contrive."

"You are very kind, Taynor Inlander."

Inlander busied himself at his computer terminal and Hook sat in the lounger waiting for the slot to disgorge crisp new money metal. Forgery of money metal was not unheard of; but in general to duplicate the complex atomic structure of the galaxy-wide money metal came as expensive as the face value of the final product. Hook had no real fears of being cheated.

Around now Hauser would be regaining consciousness and after a little fuzzy-headed cursing he'd wander around and then let out Gaines and Derning. What they would do then held the fascination of character prediction for Hook. Whatever they did, he felt with some confidence, he would still be able to re-enter the cutter and leave this star city. If they were left behind Hook felt that to be an amusing coda to the whole business.

If they came with him, of course, their whole relationship would have changed.

On balance, he decided, he'd prefer them not to accompany him.

They spelled trouble.

Lights glowed into patterns on Inlander's console and with a brief apologetic word to Hook, Inlander answered. He nodded.

"Taynor Hook, we have to clear the berthing area for the arrival of a Top-Star. We shall have to move your cutter, temporarily, of course, until berthing is completed."

There was nothing Hook could say to that. A Top-Star, as a starship of prime importance carrying passengers or freight rating the highest possible priority, took precedence over most traffic on the general interstellar runs.

"Certainly, Taynor Inlander. Do you wish –?"

"That is perfectly all right. The handling staff can move your vessel out of the way. Pray, do not disturb yourself. I have ordered refreshments to be served here."

It might have been beautifully old-fashioned and elegant, and that always attracted Ryder Hook; he could not sniff any scent of a plot here. If these Curlmen of Stellopolis wanted to steal his cargo they could do it in any of a hundred different ways. He had no reasons to suspect them of harbouring any such nefarious designs.

A red light lit up on the console.

Inlander frowned.

A service robot entered, soundless on the air-cushion carpet, trundled across bearing a silver tray loaded with refreshments. Hook helped himself to a cup and the robot poured tea. Fancy cakes and sandwiches and rocolans on porcelain presented a tempting array, and Hook helped himself. Inlander was speaking hurriedly into half a dozen microphones at once. More red lights went on. Hook sipped tea and took an interest in what the P.A. man was getting himself into.

A repeater screen from the communications centre showed robots shifting the star cutter away from her berth in the centre of the pad. They were working fast. The valves arching over the landing area rolled back. Hidden by the blaze of lighting the stars were not visible. But Hook knew they were shining away out there, eternally glittering in the whirlpool of stars. They were all his home patch.

Another repeater screen lit and displayed vectors and velocities, closing speeds and estimated time elapses. Hook absorbed them without conscious volition, as one reads print on any and everything without realising one is reading. The picture they formed flowered full in his mind.

"By the Curl of Curls!" said Inlander, and his languid pose vanished. He started to shout a string of orders.

Those constantly shifting strings of readouts were being repeated from the Top-Star closing Stellopolis and from the monitors on the city. The two sets did not match. The starship was swinging in on a direct touchdown course and was running a clear hundredth of a second out of phase. A mere hundredth of a second, when translated into terms of steel and metalloy converging under the momentum of thousands of tons of mass meeting millions of tons of mass, would mean absolute disaster. The starship was booming into a collision which the instruments showed clearly. Yet – the starship captain was speaking from another screen with a quietness of the professional making an approach which indicated quite clearly he was totally unaware of the true situation.

Other people's troubles were anathema to Hook in the ordinary way. But he knew where he was sitting and he knew what a Top-Star coming in out of phase like this could do. He stood up quickly as Inlander cut himself into the direct circuit to the incoming ship.

"Stellopolis P.A. to *Asshendahl*! You're out of phase! Captain, you have ten seconds to match. Pull back!" Inlander's languidness had all gone; he was raving. "*Pull back!*"

Starship captains were a special breed of human beings, and Top-Star captains were the best of the bunch. The captain of *Asshendahl* did not stop to argue, to say that his control readings indicated to him he was coming in on a perfect course. Immediately he initiated a control sequence that would pull speed off the approach at once. He would know a real emergency faced him and his ship and he would be prepared to have his gigantic vessel temporarily afloat in free fall and thus vulnerable around the star city, and also, into the bargain, wasting money, without further question. A lesser man, a man more confident in his own superiority as against the advice of others, might have argued. The Top-Star captain reacted instantly.

Hook liked that.

The screen over Inlander's head now lit up with a direct optical view of the starship. She was a big one. She was pictured head on and spearing into Stellopolis, and Hook was immediately reminded of a shark bearing down on him, mouth agape, nose thrust forward, tearing in to shred him between those merciless jaws.

Hook knew the Top-Star would never pull back in time.

Absolute bedlam erupted from the speakers. Alarm lights flashed continuously. A maniacal gong began to clamour.

Inlander span away from his controls.

"Too late!" he screamed. He saw Hook, as though unaware that he'd been there all the time. "Get away! Get away!"

Now the star ship filled the screen. Now her prow vanished off the edges. Now that long snout nosed forward, larger and larger. That proboscis should have made gentle contact with the flexible extension of the berth where Hook's star cutter lay. Down the treads would come the passengers into star city.

But now that long stinger speared into the city like a sword of destruction.

Only moments before Hook had been sitting quietly sipping tea and eating cakes, waiting for his money.

Now the smashing noises of total catastrophe burst about him. The overhead collapsed. The walls of glassite and steel alike crumpled and split. The floor heaved and Inlander flew helplessly through the air, to smash headfirst through his panels and emerge on the far side trailing transistor beaded taped wiring, spraying components, shrieking.

Hook held on.

The far wall splintered and burst. He felt the shock tremble through the floor. Through the savaged opening the end of the starship's probe ruptured its way past metalloy and steel, draped with framing, crumpling under the succession of shocks, driving ponderously on, bearing down on Ryder Hook.

The deadly hiss of escaping air shrieked past.

The whole berthing area had been punctured.

That deck had been laid open to space as though by the random slice of a gigantic scalpel.

Loose objects lifted and were whirled outwards.

And among the debris being flung out into space went Ryder Hook, cursing the bunch of womb-regurgitants who couldn't even berth a ship competently.

CHAPTER THREE

THAT rushing gale of escaping air whirled around Ryder Hook. Scattered chunks of debris, loose raffles of wiring and splintered metalloy, tables and chairs, filing systems, a repeater computer terminal erupting and spraying valuable components, a few screaming people tumbled head over heels, all swept in the blustering stream of air outwards.

The Top-Star had come to rest wedged into the flank of star city. Her proboscis had snapped off, exposing a skeleton of construction members entangled with the construction members of the berthing area. The chaos, the noise, the shriek of people and the shriek of escaping air built up a bedlam of insanity. A fire had caught a grip where cables had ruptured and the smashing passage of the air fanned the flames into long evil streamers before they died.

Hook caught a stanchion in a grip that would not yield before the metalloy stanchion itself broke. He looked back. In a few seconds emergency doors would slam across. The whole city would be programmed to seal itself against any wound that might open a part of itself to space. When that happened the air would exhaust and that would be the end.

Hook saw he had no chance to get back into the deeper recesses of star city before the valves closed.

He was trapped in the smashed area, isolated from the safety within. He could still breathe, dragging in lungfuls of air as it whistled past; but that wouldn't last long.

The one eighth artificial gravity cut. In free fall the departure of air and objects speeded up.

He saw a woman spreadeagled, her hair a streaming mass

of vipers' tongues around her, her face distraught, go whirling past. There was nothing he could do. The snout of the starship flailed back in the gale. The stanchion leaned as pressure built up.

Inlander had disappeared.

With a mockery as cruel as it was unnecessary a long striking stream of money-metal flew past. He ducked out of the way; that would puncture him like buckshot. And – that damned money was his! His own money, ejected from the slot of the terminal, whipped up and sucked out and pouring out into space. Hook cursed. There was no-one out there who could use money.

He took a firm grip of the stanchion, aimed himself for the Top-Star snout, and pushed off.

He barely made it.

At the last minute as he went sprawling in the air rush helter-skelter he got a hand around a jagged edge of metalloy. The force of his body sucked outwards and the sharpness of that edge should have lacerated his hand, probably have severed his fingers completely. He felt the edge digging in, and he grunted, and heaved, and got a black boot up over the edge and so hauled himself up into the distorted round of the starship's snout.

One thing, when Rocket Consortium Interstellar had monkeyed with his body, and exchanged some of his constituent atoms and molecules for living crystal metals, they'd at least given him a body that he could call on to do things denied to a normal human being. He dived in free fall down the snout and fetched up against a crumpled bulkhead beyond.

If his gamble did not pay off he was dead; but he would never give up, not even when they slipped him into space in his oxygen bottle, consigned to the stars.

A man lay sprawled against the inner edge of the bulkhead, sucked flat by the rush of air, unable to move.

Hook first looked at the telltales above the lintel of the lock leading back into the ship.

They glowed an intermittent amber, an indication that they had been caught in midcycle and were waiting for an override order.

Hook felt in the mood for giving orders – orders that would save his skin.

There were four other people trapped in this little shattered space, held against the metal walls. But they were dead, and so could not concern Hook. One had been a most lovely girl, clad in gauzy draperies and strings of jewels, with flame-coloured hair ablaze with gems. Now she lay with her head smashed in and blood and brains sticking to that gorgeous hair and streaming out in the wind bluster. With her and holding her waist lay the body of an elderly man whose bluff and stocky build and face – although dead – of dominant power showed he'd been a Krifman. Tough, rough bastards of the Galaxy, the Krifmans; but this one was as dead as the dandy who sprawled next to him, his face vacant and the top of his head missing.

Only the one young man remained alive. His eyes pleaded with Hook. He tried to speak and the air shrieked in his mouth. His blue eyes rolled towards the airlock with those flickering amber lights.

Hook guessed he was trying to say the lock was jammed.

Ryder Hook could not allow a stupid jammed lock to prevent him from getting into the starship. There'd be air in the ship. There was precious little out here, and in a second or two all that would be gone as the valves thunked shut deep in star city, sealing off this wound to space.

A clanking succession of blows resonated from the far side of the lock. Someone in there was trying to force the valves closed.

You couldn't blame them. They wanted to block off the escape of air in the same way star city had shut off this leaching injury.

Hook stared at the lock. The type was quite normal. He put his fingers, gripping with a hawk-talon fierceness, around the edge of metal. He pulled. He put out some power, some force, some of the incredible energy the RCI Powerman Project had given him. He'd not asked to go on that project with any ideas in his young head; he'd just been selected and had gone and they'd played with his body and found out what they needed to know and then they'd tossed him aside so that they could go on to create their Boosted Men. The 'they' of all this were long gone from the galactic scene, for the Boosted Men had taken over RCI. But their handiwork remained.

Ryder Hook, who was not a hundred percent Boosted Man, who was merely a normal man with an unusual body and mind, got his fingers around the jammed airlock valves – and pulled.

The metal shrieked as it dragged back.

He humped the valve just wide enough to slip through and was halfway in when he turned, remembering the youngster plastered up against the inner face of the shattered bulkhead. If the youngster could have screamed in the wind roaring past his mouth he would have done so; as it was he could only gulp at the rushing air, desperately trying to get enough into his lungs to keep alive.

Hook cursed himself for a sentimental fool.

Even as he started back the wind rush subsided.

From a blustering gale the air dropped to a whining moan and then a hideous and chilly silence.

Hook sucked in a huge lungful of the departing air, dived for the lad, got him around the waist, hauled him up. He went in through the gap between valve and architrave like a weasel, flung the youngster onto the deck, whirled, put his shoulder and hands against the valve – and thrust.

His booted feet slipped, caught a grip on the corrugated floor. There was practically no air left now. Cold smashed down. He pushed and pushed and the metal caught and gave and then, soundlessly, crashed back. Hook gave the valve a final thrust. Without a pause he leaped for the far valve, got his hands around the manual wheel, span it around so fast the spokes blurred.

Air gushed in.

Frost disappeared from the walls, dissipating. The stinging sensations of agony in Hook's eyes and nose went away. He put his head into the gush of air and, warmed, he felt the clean sweet stuff pouring into his lungs.

Then he shoved the lad into the air flow.

By the time the lock was filled and he could open the far

door the lad had babbled on about how grateful he was and how terrible this was, and Hook although not having to slap him around the face to quieten him down, had had quite enough of the fulsomeness of it all. The youngster, who said his name was Bolan Cater, laboured under the misapprehension that Hook had been risking his life to save the lad from death. Hook knew that a Bolan was a title of some sort. But for Ryder Hook lords and ladies had always been a kind of sour joke in a galaxy that cared not one whit for them or their kind. A Bolan would suffocate as unpleasantly as a slave without air.

Hook shoved the far valve open.

Half a dozen uniformed personnel of the starship's crew stood back. They carried wrenches and electronic probes and had clearly been trying to get the valves shut. Air still whistled past, escaping through the gaps and between the crumpled rims of the far door. The crew did not look pleased.

"How the hell did you get here?" demanded the man in charge, the second officer, to judge by the insignia on his white uniform.

"You were trying to shut me out," said Hook in his ugly way.

"We have to close down the valves –" The second officer quite clearly was at a complete loss. Here he was trying to do his duty after this terrible catastrophe, and strange and ugly great bastards were breaking in through the very airlocks he was trying to close down!

"You shut me out," said Hook. "And you shut out Bolan Cater –"

A woman's voice lifted in a shriek at this. In a swirl of parting crewmen a woman rushed forward and clasped Cater in her arms. She wore a lightweight spacesuit, with the helmet thrown back and collapsed out of the way, ready for instant use. She had been kitted up against disaster, just in case. Now she hugged Cater to her, smothering him with kisses.

"Bunji! Oh, Bunji! I thought you were dead! Oh, my darling boy! You have come back –"

"Mother! Let me up!"

Bolan Cater was still young enough to feel embarrassment at public display of affection. After a few years of the viciousness of the galaxy he'd be grateful for any affection that came his way.

The woman held young Bunji Cater fast and stared up at Hook. She was good-looking. Not beautiful, although the strengths of her face lay in the firm line of jaw and the clarity of her eyes. Her hair had been gathered back and severely knotted, ready for the space helmet. She looked a woman accustomed to having her own way, and yet she was alive and warm-blooded, and Hook fancied there was no play-acting in her reactions at the sight of her son miraculously restored to life.

"You and Dondar and the others – out in the probe – you were dead! The officers told me. After the accident no-one could be alive out there!" She glared wildly up at the second officer. "You said so! No air – no air –"

The second officer did not know what to say.

Hook said: "There was air. Now there is not. And unless this curd seals the locks properly there'll be no air in the ship."

The second officer shot Hook a glare of venomous hostility which Hook, glaring back, returned with interest.

Then he turned aside. Here he was descending to puerilities of this nature, outglaring some miserable little starship officer who no doubt was already shaking in his spaceboots at the enormity of what he had done. For, let there be no mistake, Hook understood the situation. A Bolan had been left out to die, and his mother had pleaded, and had been told there was no hope. And then some black bastard had wrenched open the air lock valves and carted the youngster in, safe and alive, and made the starship expertise and the starship's officers look a bunch of gonils.

No wonder Hook was glared at! And, too, no wonder that Cater's mother, Terifia, after she could tear herself away from her son, took a great interest in Hook, and held his arm, and insisted he go with her and Bunji Cater to her staterooms whilst the mess was cleared away from the Top-Star's nose and they could go into Stellopolis.

Hook, had he been a man given to grinning, would have grinned then. As it was, being human, he chuckled a trifle.

Interstellar travellers expected certain minimum standards of comfort in the ships they patronised. Here, in *Asshendahl,* the standard of comfort approached sybaritic luxury. Of all the various devices for making an interstellar flight on real time pass pleasantly here in *Asshendahl,* Hook was most taken by the clever adaption of Vin Reenurm's process for sensory enhancement. The lady Terifia's suite of cabins had been extensively wired for various sensory impressions, the controls were discreet, changing of requirements being handled by eye-movements in sequence, and the general effect was at once tasteful and highly effective.

"Oh, yes, Taynor Hook," said the lady Terifia, graciously, ushering Hook in, nodding for the serving robots to rush forward in all their plastic and metalloy servility. "I demand absolutes in life. Absolute comfort. Absolute loyalty. Absolute –"

She paused, and her son said: "What, mother. Love?"

"Oh, Bunji! You've given me enough frights for one day. You'll come of age in just one week." From the way she spoke Hook knew she meant a week terrestrial; Stellopolis employed a chronology that equated a week of their time to about eight days terrestrial. "After that you may be as rude to me as you wish. But –" And here the lady Terifia's voice sharpened. "Until then, Bunji, dear, mind your manners."

For all the horror of his experience, Bunji Cater had got over it quickly enough, and Hook suspected a great deal of his mother's power and force of personality had spilled over into him. His father might have been interesting, too . . .

The robots dispensed their services. The lady Terifia reclined in a lounger, letting her robes fall gracefully about her figure. Hook spared her two glances. Each time she still looked good. She, for her part, was perfectly aware of the picture she made, negligently leaning on an elbow, propped against static air cushions, the light brilliant on her jewels, the discarded lightweight spacesuit deftly removed and disposed of by the robots. Hook felt pleasure at the sight of her; and yet he could see her legs were fattish for their length, and he wondered why she'd not bothered to have them tailored. Cosmetic surgery was so commonplace a fact of life in the galaxy of the hundred and first century as to arouse comment when those who could afford it did not do so.

Apart from her legs, which Hook – being the ungraceful galactic adventurer he was would call short and fat if called upon to describe them – the lady Terifia was seemingly a most nicely fitted-together representative of the female section of Homo sapiens. She did have a smile that could be used in a variety of ways, to charm and to chill; Hook knew all about that. He wondered about her; but she was to him merely a woman, giving him shelter whilst the techs got the ship once more into communication with star city.

He could make polite conversation with the best of them when he had to.

"I just cannot understand how you managed it, Taynor Hook. Really, it is quite beyond me."

"It is all a blur now," said Hook. He was not prepared to allow this woman a single millimetre entrance to any of his secrets. No-one had entry there – not even, to his shame, Shaeel, who was perhaps the only real friend he possessed in the galaxy. "I just opened the air lock and helped Bunji through."

"You did that, Hook!" Bunji Cater was prepared to go on a hero-worshipping spree. This filled Hook with distaste. "You just bashed the valve open!"

"If you say so."

There were men in the galaxy who would give a very great deal to be situated where Hook was now. Here he was, sitting comfortably in the private staterooms of a great lady, with her son, the Bolan, on the very best of terms, drinking and talking and clearly quite able to ask for outrageous favours and receive them. Here was where some very good business might be done for those whose business in the galaxy was business.

Space and the great gulfs between the stars had powers to bring grandeur to a man's talk as well as feebleness of utterance against the great dark. Some people reacted in similar non-rational ways when confronted with other people who had by trick or evolution or greed acquired themselves a title or a rank or a position that, in their own estimation, placed them above the common herd; above, in this sense, again being in their own estimation. Reactions to greatness, real or fancied, told much about a man, whether he be Homo sapiens or not. Embarrassment, an over-reaction of crudity and rudeness, the expected cringing and kow-towing, all these things measured a man, just as a man was measured against the stars by the way he conducted himself in the galaxy.

Ryder Hook was perfectly polite to the lady Terifia and her son, Bunji, the Bolan Cater. Any other course would have been alien to him until they had proved themselves deserving of whatever that other course might bring. Then, why then, if necessary, Hook would deal with them as he had with Chercharon.

"The Curlmen were most anxious," Terifia said. She said this without a conscious show of pride or even of acknowledgment of her position; these things she took for granted. "They were disconsolate when we thought dear Bunji had – had – that is, before you rescued him, Taynor Hook."

"I gather the Top-Star is on your account?"

"Why, yes. I always travel Top-Star. Really, any other way of travel is so tiresome."

You should try travelling hard, frozen like a side of beef, Hook said to himself, addressing her high and mightyship. But he let her prattle on. They'd come to Stellopolis to celebrate Bolan Cater's coming of age because Stellopolis was renowned throughout this segment of the galaxy as a place of refinement and luxury and, in short, just the place to throw a party, no expense spared.

"Stellopolis had to leave their own planet when their star went nova, and they've been travelling around the galaxy ever since learning things. Oh," said Terifia, waving one hand at Hook. "Oh, yes, there are many star cities, of course, and some of them are as large as planets. But we were recommended Stellopolis – the Curlmen call their city Curl, as you know – by everyone who matters in our society." Then, just like that, out of the blue, she threw the uncatchable one at Hook. "We move in the best circles, Taynor Hook. We are with F.I.F."

She made of the statement a clear question.

Hook knew this was uncatchable in these circumstances; but he'd have a damn good try not at catching it but of chucking it back. He started to speak as the annunciator bleeped and Captain Lorton, commanding Top-Star *Asshendahl,* announced himself.

"At the moment I am not prepared to declare my allegiance to any econorg –"

And, over:

"Captain's compliments, ma'am, and may I come aboard bearing gifts?"

A robot programmed to jump when activated by the captain's speech patterns opened the door and Captain Lorton strode through, grasping in his own hands a bottle and a casket of golden filigree work. He demonstrated, by thus carrying these articles himself instead of letting a robot do the dirty work, as was usual, that he was doing the lady Terifia honour and attempting to make amends for the ghastly tragedy.

All the same, Hook noted with a little sour cynicism he found refreshing from time to time, this Captain Lorton was too damned cheerful by half.

Terifia did not rise. She turned her head and a brilliant smile illuminated her face for the captain. But she said: "No econorg, Taynor Hook? You astonish me!"

"You are looking wonderful, ma'am!" Lorton worked away at his P.R. task. A rubicund man, whose tanned face and carefully waved hair suggested a sea-faring dog, an image calculated to give a thrill of heady excitement to old ladies travelling first class with him, Captain Lorton advanced upon Terifia. He bowed, shot a look at Hook that should have melted that unregenerate on the spot, like a shot of dis-gel, and smiled at Bunji. "I am glad to see the Bolan is unharmed. A terrible business. But, happily, all over and forgotten now." He put the bottle on the table next to Terifia's lounger and extended the gold filigree box. "A token from the entire officers and crew of *Asshendahl*, ma'am, in appreciation of your passage with us!"

Bunji Cater opened his mouth and Hook knew with amused certainty that young man was going to be exceedingly impolite to the gallant captain. Hook remembered Lorton's actions when the starship was ordered to pull back, and his ready acceptance, and Hook's thoughts at the time; this was the other face of a starship captain engaged on Top-Star work. The competent space-faring officer had to be submerged in the hearty P.R. man to keep the passengers happy. Hook wasn't prepared to see a man prostitute himself like this. He rose, cutting off Bunji's remark.

"If you'll excuse me," he said. He didn't bow. He turned away, made for the door.

"Taynor Hook!" This from Terifia came almost as a wail.

"I hope to have the pleasure of your company in star city," said Hook, cutting the photo-electric eye on the door. The door opened silently. "Until then, then . . ."

He was gone before the lady Terifia had chance to say any more, long before her son Bunji, the Bolan Cater, had time to draw a fresh breath – and certainly long before Captain Lorton had time to unburden himself of his apologies and deepest hopes and best wishes and all the rest.

Darkly, Hook knew he both wanted Terifia to roast the good captain, and at the same time the captain to come as near as he could to choking off a woman who thought she was almost god-almighty.

The dichotomy tantalised him as he went off to find his way back to Stellopolis, the star city the Curlmen called Curl.

He wanted to get his hands on the money metal they owed him. Fast.

CHAPTER FOUR

ANDREWS came forward, smiling, shaking hands, saying: "Yes, Taynor Hook. I am extraordinarily glad to be able to say your cutter, although damaged, was not destroyed, and the micro-recordings all are unharmed."

"I'm glad to hear it."

The mellow yellow sun shone down through a quadruply-skinned transparent dome. Lawns spread around in segments from the bandstand in the centre, where robots pretended to be musicians, and taped music a thousand years old poured in a mellifluous flood across the park. People strolled here and there between the lawns and flower beds. Andrews, a man whose high function in star city could be ascertained only because he wore a gold ornament around his neck, and because two men in enforcer's black uniforms followed him everywhere, their hands on their gun butts, clearly was overjoyed at their good fortune.

"Our records show that the money metal owing to you was dispensed –"

"I never received it."

"That is not strange, under the circumstances. Also, I am more than happy to say, Taynor Inlander is alive. He was seriously injured and is under intensive care; but he'll be up and around again in a couple of days."

"That is good news."

"Yes."

"I never received the money metal. Everything blew apart when it was due."

Andrews frowned. He was a big and luxuriant man, with a mass of dark hair, and a nose that surgery alone kept in shape. His midriff bulged. "I cannot do a thing about the records, Taynor Hook. As far as the records show, you are paid in full."

Hook felt tired. Suddenly, just like that, he felt worn out. He'd have to fight for the filthy money they owed him, just as he was always having to fight in this damned galaxy.

"The money metal never reached me, therefore you have not fulfilled your contract."

Cheerfully-smiling Andrews did not spread his hands, apologising, diplomatic. He did not have to. What he said went. Hook had kept this off-handed appointment only because he was in the supplicant position. As for Hook himself, as a man; he was a man without a credit card, hence he was a nobody, and hence, equally hence, Andrews need not give a twopek damn for him.

Despite all this Andrews maintained that distant and careful politeness that skinned the depths of true violence of which any man in his position was capable. Andrews ran all this section of the city – call it borough, precinct, poral – and he knew his own powers.

"It has been pleasant meeting with you, Taynor Hook. We of Stellopolis are grateful for the microrecordings you have sold us. Good day to you."

With his enforcers at his back, dark and ominous, Andrews walked slowly away in that warm and friendly sunshine.

Ryder Hook looked after him, and wondered why he didn't just belt the guy across the ear.

The reason was simple. Asinine violence would get him dead very fast, and Hook wanted his due payment, not a lethal flash from an energy gun.

They'd repair his cutter. At least, they'd do that. That would conform to interstellar codes of conduct. Laws were tricky things; there were no romantic interstellar police flitting about among the stars to sort out troubles and to whom you could take your grievances. As far as Hook knew, there were no fine fancy galactic policemen. Who would pay them? Organise them? Under whose authority would they operate? Would you let another solar system or multi-system conglomerate operate an interstellar police force without wanting your share of the say-so? And as for letting the watch-dogs command themselves, that way lay another stupid and ultimately suicidal attempt at this nonsense of a galactic empire.

Had Hook belonged to an econorg or a union he would have been on the communications link immediately, and pretty soon his very own organisation would have been putting pressure on the Curls of Stellopolis. But the Curls knew he had no credit card. They knew he was a loner. They knew and took advantage of the fact that he had no-one who would help him. He could be pushed around without fear. With an econorg at his back he'd have pulled more power right away than any romantic interstellar police could have done for him. But, despite all this, Ryder Hook would remain a loner in the galaxy.

He started to get mad.

This was a silly thing to do; but he felt that dragging ache on him, and the way his brains hurt as though they were frying. All those marvellous organic implants in his skull had no part of this; and he had not activated them for some time. There would be an apparat net operating around here somewhere, keyed to the agents of some super-bureau or other. But he'd do this thing on his own. He was getting madder by the minute. Damned bunch of star-city layabouts! Wombregurgitants! He'd damn well show the gonils they couldn't push Ryder Hook about and live to brag about their prowess!

No, by God! He'd do something drastic, and the quicker the sooner.

The decision taken, Hook lost all animosity against Andrews personally. The man was just doing a job he considered to be important, and his records must show the money metal as having been paid out. That it had gone spinning and billowing out into space was not his concern. You couldn't blame the man. But Hook felt very much like blaming the city. He wanted his money. The fault of the crash had not yet been decided, and maybe there would be a whitewash job on that; all that Hook considered relevant was that he was owed money, the city had not put that cash into his hand, so he was going to do that little thing himself.

These people who called themselves Curls and who came from a planet now destroyed called Curl had called their star-wandering city Curl. You could feel sorry for them in that their original sun had gone nova and they'd had to move. That had happened to many races in the galaxy. They'd simply upped sticks and equipped their city with a number of coupled units of some standard ftl drive and taken off.

Why they had chosen to settle in orbit around this planet Voyden, second out around the star Purlon Major, perhaps no-one could know. They'd been here two hundred years terrestrial. Stellopolis extended, as Hook had earlier observed, for a good few kilometres in every direction, a thumping great mass of buildings whirling around in space. Arteries of communication linked sections, either tubed airlanes or tubed highways, with borough linked to borough by covered bridges and flexible hose-like extensions. The whole mass moved within itself, gently, as it circled in orbit, and one wouldn't bother about that when a touch on an ftl drive unit would settle everything nicely back into equilibrium once more.

Many sections lived comfortably with the standard space-style of one eighth terrestrial gravity applied to give a reassuring up and down. Other sections existed in free fall, and no doubt high jinks took place there from time to time. Yet further sections existed where the gravity was maintained at what was, relevant to Earth, one point one, and Hook gathered that this was the Curlmen's natural mode of life, inherited from their original planet. Every now and then a man wanted to feel that primordial gravity pulling on his bones and muscles; that way he might push back a trophy.

For a man like Hook – and the only men like Hook he knew of were the Novamen – who had been adapted to work as easily under nine gravities as he did under one, gravitic changes came without comment. He stomped off out of the park and avoided a gang of speedsters in their electric cars whirling down a dual-carriageway tube, watched as they soared up in an arching loop to join an expressway crossing at right angles, creating a snarl of traffic, and so walked on cherishing that germ of hatred. Hook knew how to hate, all right; but also he knew the values of hatred and how non-hatred paid better dividends. Hook didn't hate these Curlmen of Stellopolis; he just wanted them to pay the money they owed him; and if they wouldn't pay voluntarily then they'd pay involuntarily.

All around him the city hummed and buzzed and clicked and bustled about its multifarious purposes. The people here kept busy, maintaining the city, organising resources, sending to the planetary surface of Voyden for raw materials and venting their wastes back. The folk here had a lot to do in their prime purpose of seeking and finding luxury and pleasure. There were many planets and star cities in the galaxy whose prime objective was to find pleasure. Hedonists of the galaxy, they performed essential work. Hook knew that. For him, going grimly off to get the money he was owed, they would have only contempt. Very well, then, contempt it would be.

A bank?

One of the many tentacles of the business power of any of the many econorgs who had outlets here?

Possibly.

He didn't want to have to push his luck and go for a hard-shell outlet, where there would be goons and radiation-fields and homotropic snoopers and a varied arsenal of the defensive apparatus designed to prevent one econorg from doing down another.

F.I.F. were well represented here. So were Interstell Imp and Sieur Stel and a dozen others. There was no RCI agency here on Stellopolis, and Hook felt cheated because of that. RCI was dominated by the Boosted Men, and had they an agency here it was almost certain a Novaman would be here also, and then Hook's task would have been immeasurably easier.

Too bad . . .

Out of sorts as he was, he needed a lift.

In the end he selected an agency of GCC, for he had the idea the Boosted Men were infiltrating this particular econorg and even so lowly a thing as a robbery on the scale he contemplated might impede their schemes, if only for a heartbeat in galactic time.

He walked smoothly and sedately past the main entrance.

Even on a star city the econorgs protected themselves with a zealous care for their own rights. The roof bristled with armament suitable for inter-dome work; no doubt the city bosses would not allow weapons there that would blow chunks out of the city screening. The front door presented a formidable obstacle to anyone who sought to enter without a GCC wrist credit card to flash at the scanners.

The block rose from the highest street level sheer for a hundred metres. All below that level, and Hook checked, there were six other levels, radiating a cross-hatching of tube-ways. The walls were predictably sheer there, also. Only above that hundred metre mark were windows let into the metalloy fabric. Sparse for the first five hundred metres, they increased in numbers higher up the building. From that weapons-bristling roof a tower some thousand metres thick rose to join the dome. Beyond the dome, mistily visible as a black smear, a spire projected into space. So they had their own berthing facilities. To be expected. GCC were pretty big in the galaxy these days.

Hook checked everything most carefully, and waited until the orbit of star city carried it past the curve of the planet below. For a few hours a kind of twilight night would fall, as the limb of the planet occluded the sun. Lights sparkled up all over this section of Stellopolis. Those lights in their fairy strings and blazing coruscations must make a pretty picture from space. Hook, staring hungrily up, saw them only as giving him a little chance against the goons of GCC.

The city bosses of Stellopolis would have to reimburse GCC, if things went right. They had power, had these men of star city, to be very nasty to agencies who did not do things the way the city bosses requested; and equally an agency of a great econorg could spread the word and a star city would suddenly fall away in importance if it failed to honour its debts to an econorg.

Checks and balances; these were the things that kept the galaxy running, not brute force and armadas of space war-ships.

Not that there were not the occasional upsurgings of cultures new in the galaxy who thought they could send fleets of conquering starships out to carve empires for themselves... They would be quickly taught the error of their ways; but for a time life around them in the galaxy would be highly unpleasant.

The last little money metal he had left he spent on a good meal in a restaurant far removed from the GCC agency he had selected as his target. Robots vended a tasty dish of Kichan roasted meats, served in a wine sauce, with those tender little bamboo-shoots that had never grown in Earth's China, and Hook allowed himself a little luxury here, considering that star city existed to dispense that commodity. He drank tea, detesting coffee, and exchanged a few words with the couple in the adjoining booth.

"Going to the Stelldrome, taynor?"

"Can you recommend it?" Hook wouldn't admit he didn't know what was playing.

The girl laughed, displaying a low neckline and a transparent blouse to some advantage. "Oh, yes! A troupe of automatons who make no pretence at aping humans. They are droll! We've been anxious to go all week."

"I might look in. I hope you enjoy the show."

"We will, taynor, we will."

Hook paid with his money metal, and drew a puzzled frown from the couple, who simply flashed their credit cards. Hook made himself laugh after the fashion of a dizzy luxer. A luxer who sought sybaritic delights with all a hedonist's application was completely at home on Stellopolis. "A wager, friends. Can a man live a whole week and not use his credit card?"

They laughed. It was the kind of wager they understood.

"You'll never do it," said the man.

"But we wish you good luck," said the girl.

Clearly, they thought him an idiot to take on so difficult a bet.

During this meal and as he sauntered back ready for the darkness to fall as the limb of the planet occulted the sun, Hook very carefully opened out those organic implants in his skull.

He listened out to the galaxy.

When he'd been ordered to volunteer, as a member of Earth's Armed Forces, and as Sergeant Jack Kinch had become the most notorious assassin in the galaxy, he had used these circuits in his head to keep alive, to give him information, to keep contact with control. He had not done a great deal of work for EAS; what he had done had been enough. Even today, so long afterwards, there were planetary bosses and heads of econorgs who trembled in their skins at the sound of the name Jack Kinch.

Nowadays, Ryder Hook was plain Ryder Hook, galactic wanderer; he had put away Jack Kinch for ever. But, as now, every once in a while he keyed open the circuits EAS had implanted in his skull and tuned in to the nearest apparat net.

That 'nearest' of course meant different things in different contexts. He might not be able to pick up the local police enforcers' net as they controlled their activities in the star city; but his EAS organic implants were designed to be activated by a centre perhaps so many parsecs away that normal ftl radio links might attenuate. He listened out carefully.

His brain could by straight forward induced coil circuits think him through the frequencies. He skipped along, recognising the chatter as a busy working day for the espionage boys, for the counter-espionage people, for the many different outfits in the galaxy who wished to place their own operatives in certain positions so that they might do for them something probably lethally nasty to their opponents.

The chatter filling his head provided a cross-section of what was going on in the galaxy between those various shadowy organisations who existed on the fringes of polite society. Information gathering, justice enforcement, espionage and counter-espionage, straightforward domination and control of others, all these people made their living without surfacing into the light of overt politics and day-to-day living. They inhabited the half-world of the galaxy, a half-galaxy Jack Kinch had known and detested.

He picked up a control centre who had an operative aboard a starship with orders to assassinate an important passenger, and moved on to another who were controlling an operative at this moment feeling his way through a darkened arsenal on a permanently frozen moon to steal the secrets of life and death manufactured there. He recognised many of the controls. Deliberately, he didn't go near any EAS frequencies. EAS had outfitted him with these organic transplants and they had at the time perhaps the best techniques in the known galaxy. He had been equipped to eavesdrop on other apparat nets without their knowledge. He could insinuate himself along the tenuous paths occupied by an operative and, like a ghost, pace the task being performed.

This was not telepathy. Oh, it was nearly that, of course, brain patterns amplified by organo-electronic means and flung the millions of kilometres between the stars, light-year conversations, parsec long instructions; but telepathy – no. This was scientific methods adapted to a human brain and giving that human brain the power of near-instantaneous communication with another human brain across the galaxy.

Hook ran through for an operative signing off.

When he found what he sought and heard that ghostly whisper in his brain saying: "That's all, Flo. The stuff's on its way to you by star-packet. Give my best to Charlie," he recognised an apparat with whom he could work. The control, Flo, said: "Check, Fram. Nice one. You'll be in contact."

Hook exerted his power.

He over-rode the last few words from Fram, saying: "Flo? Give me a quick rundown on this, will you?"

He looked at the GCC building.

Flo said: "Hold it a minute – there – coming up – *now.*"

Over Hook's retinas appeared the projected semblance of the GCC building. He could see layer by layer through the building, as masonry and metalloy stripped away under the gaze of the instrument telltales under the control of Flo's console assistants. He'd tuned into a big net, then. Nice. He saw the GCC building in true perspective, for the head-up display against his retinas presented the building in focus. A check very quickly established the main outlines of the defensive system.

Flo said: "You break in there, they'll crucify you."

She accepted him as one of the operatives employed by her

own apparat net – for how could anyone else speak to her over her systems?

Hook said: "Red section want an assist, Flo. Call me Red, if you have to. That place has to be busted."

"You're buying trouble."

"That's the business."

"That window on the – um – sixtieth floor. Checks out with a faulty alarm."

Somewhere on a planet light years away a console assistant programmed her computer and that beam of non-telepathic thought speared from the outlet and into Hook's brain, caught and identified by his organo-electronic implants, flashed up from his brain to his eyes. What he actually saw was a fluorescent orange ring suddenly encircle a window on the sixtieth floor, high up beneath the dome.

"You'll need your anti-grav pack for that one, Red."

"Don't have an ag-pak."

Flo must have been a senior controller, for she had no hesitation in saying: "What they doing over in Red section? Losing their lift? Grab an ag-pak or suction kits –"

"No chance."

"The choice is yours, soldier. We'll run you through when you're in; but you'll have to get in on your own."

Sixty floors up, a window with a faulty alarm would allow ingress. Hook cocked his head, staring up. How to get up there?

Being Ryder Hook he had the obvious answer ready.

CHAPTER FIVE

RYDER HOOK said: "Check this out."

He looked around the street level, slowly turning his body, revolving in a complete three sixty degree circle. He appeared to see the metalloy sheeting vanish and the working lifelines of star city show through. Cables and conduits, circuits and energy beams all spread out before him. He tapped into a thick cable marked with the black and white that often indicated ag-power and followed it downwards. It vanished into a lead-shielded construct situated below and dead centre of this domed section of the city.

"Check, Flo. Stay with me until I'm zeroed in."

"Check, Red. I have you."

Walking slowly and acting as just another citizen of Stellopolis, Ryder Hook descended a glideway, strode a pedway and descended again until he was near enough to the ag-generator.

He looked about again and this time he looked in order to see what normal sight would show. He was alone. He took out the Tonota Eighty. He notched it up to full power.

He must be very careful. Hook knew and approved of those cultures who refused to allow a starship passenger the possession of a powergun in space. The things were too dangerous, and the usual weapons – a dis-gel gun, a buzz-saw, a toxicator – for use in space were amply lethal enough. If he'd been running star city he'd have confiscated all energy weapons the moment they showed in the berthing area.

No matter who carried 'em.

He shot the lead shielding out.

It pyrotechnically blotted out in light and thunder all reason and all vision. The Tonota hammered on, pouring its vicious radiation and concentrated power into the heart of the ag-generator. Hook saw shielding blowing apart, saw chunks of core separating and flowing, saw a little fire begin where a fire has no reason to exist and snuffed a sideways blast across it so that the backlash of air extinguished the licking flames. He melted down the on-site controls and saw the end of the black and white cable go snaking away, lashing like a cobra, spitting sparks.

He pushed gently against the pavement.

In free fall he drifted up past the pedways and glideways down which he had just walked.

Alarm sirens keened. Automatic fans span into blurs as they came on to circulate the atmosphere.

Hook soared up through the interstices of the interleaved walkways and drifted comfortably to the top street level. He said: "Here we go, Flo."

He jumped.

In free fall he went soaring along the flank of the GCC agency buildings. Because of his ancestry Hook's senses attuned to the assumption that the building lay below him and that he flew along it like a bird over the countryside. To an onlooker standing on the pavement below with his head pointed to the overhead dome, Hook would have appeared to be walking up the side of the building.

Every now and then he pushed off afresh, for the distance was great enough for a simple single massive jump to bring him hard against the dome with momentum enough to break through, given the extraordinary powers of his body.

At the window on the sixtieth floor he hauled up on the sill.

Flo's voice in his head said: "I must say you don't mess about." There was naked admiration there. Hook grunted and bashed the window in.

Although alarms were sounding all over this domed area no alarm so much as cheeped from the window.

Hook eased in. He turned to look down, for now the floor of the room gave a normal perspective to the view, and saw star city techs flailing along towards the smoking crater. That smoke was being whipped away by the fans and sucked off into disposal chutes. People were crowding around and flying up and generally congregating to see the excitement. Hook went back to the room and padded across to the far door. The room's darkness was no impediment to him, for Flo had coupled in a pair of infra-lux scanners and he could see as well as in daylight. He went into the corridor and headed for the banking section. He carried the Tonota in his hand. His face would have scared a gargoyle.

Finding the banking outlet was easy.

Breaking into it presented a considerable problem; but with Flo operating from her agency light years away to guide him, Hook could see the interior wiring of the alarms, could short-circuit the easiest and blow holes in the more intractable. He dealt mercifully with the half dozen guards who arrived on the scene. The Tonota, being an Eighty and therefore capable of doing the holocaust-destruct work he had just employed it on, was also capable when fined down of delivering a sweet-dreams punch, a paralyser. Hook put the guards to sleep gently and went back to opening up the ready-money safes. They had been sealed for the night, of course; but as close to money metal as this Ryder Hook wouldn't wait for a long-drawn out tumbler – sniffing and turning technique. He blasted the corner off the nearest safe, kicked the hot metal aside, trampled around a bit and then began scooping money metal.

"You have dilly assignments in Red section," said Flo.

"Check."

"I read heavy breathing, rapid heart-beat, concealed foot-step vibration, coming from your left rear."

Hook whirled, triggered the Tonota, sent the last goon into sweet-dreams.

"Thanks, Flo."

Now had he been operating in fast time, as a Boosted Man, he'd have picked up all the signals Flo had read from the display boards of her console, channelled in through Hook's ears, long before. As it was, he was a mere Homo sapiens ordinariensis.

He took exactly the amount of money metal owed him.

This was a stupid thing to do.

But, being Ryder Hook, he did it anyway. And then, after he'd thought about it for perhaps a microsecond, he blew off the corner of four more ready money safes. A consignment of micro-happenings had spaced in yesterday, and after they were cleared through GCC's agency, they'd be paid for in money metal. The star-faring race who'd brought them in, the so-called star-merchants, had wanted money on the nail. Otherwise Hook would not have turned over so much ready cash. He let it go drifting about in free fall, admiring the way the metal bills flashed in the subdued lighting.

"You havin' fun, Red?"

"Orders, Flo."

He caught a harder edge to control's words.

With the money metal safely stashed into his inside belt pouch, his Tonota ready, Hook took off. He listened in his head to an instant play-back of Flo's last words, and again he caught that sharpness.

The people on night duty within the agency had mostly gone streaming out to gawp at the ag-generator wreckage, and those guards Hook had met now slumbered. He felt it redundant to make his way back to the sixtieth floor. All the alarms might go off in one great burst – after he'd departed. He took the precaution of burning the air after him, with the Tonota set on wide-angle and half-aperture, feeling the draught rushing in to replace what he incinerated. In free-fall conditions the calculations were interesting; but all he was concerned with there was to dispose of his body residuals. When the forensic sniffers went to work they'd have nice fresh clean air to work on containing no trace of Ryder Hook.

Flo worried him.

She worked for a big apparat net, and he'd picked on them for that reason. But he didn't like that last edgy tone in her voice. As far as Hook knew – and he could always be wrong – there were less than half a dozen controls with operatives capable of cutting into another net. And of them all – again so Hook believed – Earth's Armed Services were the best. He'd given EAS a soldier's farewell, and wanted no more to do with them. He was grateful, in a twisted back-handed kind of way, for what they'd plumbed into his cranium. But he was on his own now. If Flo's outfit, too, had the capacity to cut in, the idea wouldn't shock her as it would a normal control who firmly believed the non-telepathic but surrogate-telepathic links were inviolable.

Flo said: "You said you were with Red section, Red. You've done a nice job –"

Hook wasn't listening.

He shut off those organo-electronic circuits in his head so fast it sounded like the clap of doom.

He wondered by how many micro-seconds he'd baulked the flash of killing energy Flo's superiors had flung at him.

He told himself to remember to check up on Flo and her apparat later on, find out what they thought of Red, if he could.

He blew the third floor window of a lady's lavatory out into a well. He soared out, pushed off and sailed easily over the opposite wall, let himself fall by easy stages to the street level.

By this time the Tonota was discreetly back in its holster. People were skylarking about, leaping up and somersaulting in free fall and as the limb of the planet slid past and away in a running bead-like procession of burgeoning light the annunciators came on warning of resumption of normal artificial gravity. There was a five minute warning so that anyone who'd lightly jumped off a bridge in the abandon of free-fall conditions wouldn't be smacked down to the ground in a jelly of blood.

Hook noticed the way the Stellopolis' techs brought the gravity on smoothly, and he felt the smack of his booted feet against the metalloy decking as he walked. He was clear of the GCC building and the area and well on his way to the P.A. berth where, Andrews had assured him, his star cutter was repaired and ready to go.

What he had just done was according to the laws of this star city highly illegal. He had committed a criminal act. He had harmed no one. The guards would wake up feeling no worse than before. He had destroyed property; but in an interstellar culture artefacts of far greater importance and complexity than a light-duty ag-generator were routinely lost and retailored or recycled. Accordingly replacement would be minimal. In the view of a man without protection in the galaxy what he had done merited a simple answer; he had taken what belonged to him, no more, no less. Relativity played a part here, of course; what he was owed that could not be paid in money had counted in the equation.

Now he would take the cutter – which was his only because he'd stolen it from the Boosted Men – and space out.

Getting away from Stellopolis would be a pleasure.

He didn't blame the Curlmen; they were only acting as almost all the peoples of the galaxy would act in the same circumstances.

The shape of the planet Voyden swung past over his head now as star city pirouetted in its orbit. He could see the swirl of clouds and the sheen off the seas as the sun struck in at a low angle from its recent eclipse. The Curlmen had settled their star city into a relatively low orbit and the planet covered a vast expanse of the city's skyview. Hook was accustomed to having enormous balls of matter apparently hanging unsuspended in space above his head; for a planetary culture accustomed only to a moon as large, say, as old Earth's, such a vision would be monstrous, frightening, awe-inspiring.

As he looked, relishing the spectacular sight of that massive planet, glowing in misty white and blue highlights, sombre in green and brown shadows, glittering with the sun off water, Hook saw the smoothly deliberate approach of a ship. She drew in matching orbits and velocity and then vanished beyond the tower of a department store, heading for the berthing area. Hook walked on. Presently, looking up again, he saw the discharge of waste matter from star city, the elongated blobs of darkly shining stuff spinning and vanishing away to fall at last somewhere on the surface of the planet of Voyden.

A kind of peace enveloped him and, recognising that old devil tiredness overtaking him, he could yet relish the ease of it and the blessedness of the sleep to come. Down past a cross-street where electric traffic moved silently and effortlessly, clean in the star city atmosphere, he saw the entrance to the berthing area.

A bare half-dozen paces down the side-street brought him

abreast a doorway. From the doorway, guns in their hands, stepped Locum Hauser and Walton Gaines. Hook stopped. People were walking past those half-dozen paces off; but they would only see three men talking peacefully.

Gaines said: "We've been waiting for you, Hook."

Hauser said: "I'll blast him down now, Walt."

The dominant emotion in Hook's mind was contempt – blazing, scathing, merciless contempt for himself. Here he'd been sauntering along, maundering about the beautiful view of the planet, feeling tired, looking forward to a shower and a sleep; and – now! He was an idiot of idiots! If ever he forgot again the prime directive of life in this galaxy, he'd be dead. There was no time to relax. Relaxation was strictly for those with credit cards and money and guards and enforcers to do their will. A simple galactic wanderer had no time letting his mind wander from the main course of life.

"Hi, Gaines, Hi, Hauser," he said. He couldn't summon a smile, so he managed to lift a corner of his upper lip.

Both Gaines and Hauser regarded that as a symptom of fear.

They were wrong; but the miniscule amount of time they'd spent coming to that conclusion stood between them and an instant pressing of triggers. They clutched energy guns and they'd use 'em, and the devil take what happened in the path of the twin blasts.

"You killed Cher-charon, Hook. That was a bad thing to do."

Hook rubbed his head. He moved his hands very carefully.

"You tried to kill me, so did Cher-charon. What do you want now?"

"We want what's ours. Where's the cash from the sale? Come on Hook, we know you got paid off."

"All the money metal was sucked into space."

"Give!" Gaine's gun twitched.

There was no chance of jumping them; they were old hands at this and held their weapons far enough away so that at his first tensing to spring they could fire.

He was not in a Boosted state. He was just an ordinary man

with some very extraordinary powers. He was no superman. He had to remember that . . .

"Where's Happy?" He spoke with the casual thoughtlessness of an acquaintance asking another of a third. He sounded artless.

"Money metal, Hook! *Give*!"

They were going to kill him. They were very sure of that. Hook dug into the inside pouch and produced the money metal he had removed from the GCC agency's banking outlet. Both Gaines and Hauser looked interested.

"Sucked into space! Haw, you gonil, Hook."

They had him angled, bracketed. He could deal with one of them, probably; whilst he did that the other would shoot. Hook knew enough about them and their kind to know the shooter wouldn't worry if his pal was caught in the blast.

Again, he said: "Where's Happy?"

"He'll get his share. Don't you fret. Come on, hand it over." Gaine's eyes fixed on the money metal in Hook's hands.

What Ryder Hook had to do now pained him. There was no way of saving the money and his skin. Of the two, important though the money was, it meant nothing compared to the importance he attached to his own skin. So he would have to use the cash to save himself. Again he weighed the chances of jumping them both and again he decided against. Insane risks he would take; but not this kind of suicide.

He riffled the money metal.

"Give, Hook, you curd!" Hauser's eyes, too, fixed on the flashing bills passing between Hook's hands.

Hook took a pace back.

That made five.

Five in normal walking paces, that was. Say one and a bit doing what he would have to do.

The bills riffled through his hands. He set himself, without altering the rhythm of the flashing metal. He poised with one foot anchored for a thrust, the other barely touching the metalloy paving. He spoke cheerfully.

"Sure, Gaines. Sure, Hauser. You c'n have the money. You're a pair of creeps, anyway. I bet Happy don't get his."

He held the money out and twisted one hand slightly and

the scintillating spray of bills fluffed, spilled, and sprayed outwards. Two pairs of eyes fastened leech-like on the scattering money.

One and a bit leaps.

The money was still scattering, two pairs of eyes were abruptly re-focussing on the side-street, two forefingers were tightening on triggers. Hook's first leap took him to the corner and the bit flung him around. The twin blasts scorched past, scything into the street, vapourising a passing electric car and a group of passersby. The metalloy decking smoked into a long brown greasy weal.

Hook just ran flat out to the next corner, jinked twice – unnecessarily, and whipped around it.

If he knew Gaines and Hauser they were picking up money.

A siren ululated reassuringly.

The enforcers were hurrying to this spot. Some sonofabitch had been letting of a power gun and they'd want to know why. They'd tie this in with the two previous blasts, probably.

Hook straightened up his clothes and walked with the crowd to see what was going on. He was alive and he was in the clear. But he damned-well didn't have a pek to show for his night's work.

CHAPTER SIX

RYDER HOOK watched it all on the tv in Terifia's apartment.

He lounged in a comfortable knee-length robe of salafan silk, tastefully decorated with legendary monsters and caught by magneclasps about him in such a way as to reveal a modicum of his manly chest – so the sales brochures on the readout had suggested it should be worn – eating a tasty appetite-giving pre-lunch snack, and from time to time casting an appreciative glance at Terifia, who sat with her legs curled up on the opposite lounger and wearing an identical robe.

The tv showed almost all. The actual shoot-out was omitted and was replaced by a filmed recording of a ballet-troupe who'd caused a great stir a year or so before in Stellopolis. But the news media showed the chase, the steady overhaul, the grappling and the final boarding. Then the ballet, at which point Terifia rather spoiled the effect she caused by swinging her legs out and suggesting they go in to eat. Hook was hungry, right enough, even after the last few days of good food at Terifia's, and they ordered the com-robot to transfer the tv image to the dining room. The three-dimensional impression cube lit on the far wall as they sat down to a meal as marvellous as any of them had been. The story picked up again as the triumphant Stellopolis enforcers emerged from the battered cutter waving the packet of money metal. What they had done to Walton Gaines, Locum Hauser and Happy Derning was not shown.

The morality of it all made Hook aware that he was a simple human being; but it did not put him off his food.

He was more involved with the moral problem presented by this fulsome attitude of Terifia in thus taking him under her wing. She had sought him out, using a public-address system which could put anyone in touch with anyone else who was listening if they could afford to pay the city bosses for the privilege. Now she was clearly bent on conquering him. No doubt she saw in him ripe plunder. The Bolan's coming of age party was due this night as ever was, when Voyden occulted the sun, and there was going to be the biggest high jinking of any high jinks Stellopolis had seen. Hook was beginning to find out just how wealthy Terifia was. She kept a retinue of plug-uglies to maintain her isolation from the mundane herd. Hook's isolation came from outside as well as inside, these days.

"Those stupid curds," Terifia said, tapping her lips with a sensitised cloth that instantly cleansed them. "How they thought they could escape eludes me. They must have known the owner of the ship would report its loss."

"They didn't think," said Hook. He spoke in a grey and neutral tone. He wasn't proud of reporting in to the city bosses that his cutter had been stolen; but he had done so in a fit of fine civic zeal, and, lo and behold, the mystery of the GCC agency bank raid was solved.

Terifia clearly shared that opinion. She sipped at her crystal glass of telil – a drink Hook equated with a waste of money – and said: "GCC ought to pay a reward, Hook. You should claim."

Doing that would provide a laugh. Ryder Hook was a man who valued a good laugh more than most, more than a man, for example, who laughed too often and too easily.

"I don't have a credit card, Terifia. They're not likely to pay much attention to me."

"I'll damn well make them!" She sat up straight, and her features took on a rosier glow through the tan. "If I can be properly grateful to you, Hook, then so can some damn agency who're not half the size of F.I.F.!"

"You're very kind," said this Ryder Hook who was quite happy to be humble when it suited his nefarious purposes.

The news report gave way to coverage of an inter-zonal match and Terifia irritatedly snapped at her robots to switch the tv off. The wall-size three-dimensional appearance cube died and collapsed and slid away into its cupboard. Soft quarter-tone music drifted into the scented atmosphere.

"You're too pessimistic, Hook. Oh, I know you're a damn fool for not having a credit card; but –" Here an idea occurred to Terifia, and she went on: "I'll fix you up with F.I.F. When I tell 'em they'll be only too happy. Yes, that's what we'll do, Hook."

Vague ideas of sympathy for Bunji Cater, her son, crossed Hook's mind. This lady had a will of her own. Hook decided with some reservations that he'd attend the party out of mere politeness, and because the Cater family might turn nasty, and then he'd see about spacing out.

"My ship's smashed up again," he said. And then Ryder Hook made a foolish statement. "When Stellopolis has her repaired again –"

"I doubt if they'll do that, Hook. They'll claim it was no fault of theirs your ship was damaged. And they'd be right."

Then Hook saw the fatuousness of his statement.

In this man's galaxy no-one did anything for anyone else unless interest, payment or obligation indicated they should do so. That wasn't entirely true. There were selfless people still, races and combines and unions who sought only to do good. But Hook, to his sorrow, did not often space the same lanes as those.

The lady Terifia, now, was seeking to do good for Hook. There was the matter that he had rescued her son from death; but Hook summed up Terifia as a lady who would damned-well go on doing what good she could and stand from under if you got in the way.

"But," said Terifia, stretching, perfectly at ease, "if you had the power of F.I.F. behind you – why, then, Hook, you'd swing some weight when you talked with the city bosses."

Hook could recall with a frightful mental clarity the way the RCI credit-card scientists had removed the credit card neurologically implanted in his left wrist. That had been when RCI had thrown him out of their Powerman Project.

He didn't want to go through that experience again.

"I'll think about it, Terifia." He knew he was being weak –

and that was a novelty – but he felt quite certain that situated as he was now he had no wish to offend this powerful woman. At the right time he might take a very different attitude; but he could feel somnolently able to take advantage of her now. If she wanted to be a galactic do-gooder, Ryder Hook, although abhorring the idea he might be a gentleman, had no wish to deter her.

Just getting a means of transportation off Stellopolis would be a price for a bargain . . .

Later that afternoon – for Stellopolis besides running a neat eight-terrestrial-day week ran also a varying-length day and night cycle, in a diurnal rhythm originating on their home planet, now destroyed, of Curl – Hook took a new look at star city. He was as impressed as he would ever allow himself to be, and this not from any dog-in-the-manger attitude of cynicism, which set out never to be astonished; rather, he wanted always to hold a little of himself in reserve.

Stellopolis flowered among the stars.

Crowds of brilliantly-dressed people flipped and tripped and cavorted along the brilliantly lit avenues. Anything the heart could desire could be obtained, and all flavoured with the peculiar Curlmen's-mystique of luxury. From the stark necessity of having to lift a city and equip it with ftl drive engines and take off into the stellar night, the Curlmen had developed a way of life that perfectly attuned them to living eternally in space. Out of emergency they had created beauty. Like fireflies of the dark spaces, the avenues and tubeways glowed against the night. Fire-flies, fire-light, fire-clad, laughter and abandon and joyousness spread throughout star city. Cares were sloughed away. Wine flowed, catching the lights, as it poured unceasingly from stainless-steel fountains, feathering, ruby-red, diamond-yellow, flowing and flowing into the sculptured ceramic basins. Gaily-dressed throngs circulated, dipping tubes into the never-ending flow of wine, sipping and laughing. Bright eyes glittered through the eye-slits of facial-masks hewn to shapes more grotesque than a planetary-bound culture could conceive. Shrill laughter racketted over the piazzas. Men chased women, and girls chased boys, and everywhere the spirit of fiesta, of saturnalia, of sheer enjoyment because enjoyment was the greatest gift the Curl of Curls could bestow, spluttered and pulsed through Stellopolis.

Scenes like these might be enacted a million times over on a million planets of the galaxy – and all the millions more – but for Ryder Hook because he was in the heart of the raveup on Stellopolis then these hectic adventurings became the most important in the galaxy. No Boosted Man came near and for the time being Ryder Hook was quite prepared to abandon himself to the simple delight of living it up.

"Come on, luxers! Boil in!"

A giant grotesque in skin-tight glitter costume with swirling flittery draperies swirling as he pranced bounded across the plaza where music and laughter swayed against the night. The anti-grav pack strapped to the grotesque's back gave him airy leapings and cavortings; the black mask shone with the diamond dust of pleasure, the skirlings and swathings brought him all swivery and helter-skelter to pause before the lady Terifia.

Hook eyed the grotesque.

In all this frenetic laughter and scurryings about, in the drinking and the play, with balloons plopping and shrill shrieks of girls and lads skimming chutes into anti-grav suspended bowls of water, extra-oxygenated, scented, coloured, the grotesque for all his costume and his mask and his exaggerated mimicry struck a discordant note. Despite all his determination to relax and enjoy himself among the fun-seekers and the luxers, Hook tensed up and then relaxed into a feral waiting very different from the loose relaxation of a moment before.

"Hey, luxers! Here's the damsel herself!" The grotesque pranced before Terifia, shaking, laughing. Her bodyguards, four dark hard men from Anselm laughed, too, seeing no danger here. They were good; but this was play-time and this grotesque one of the players.

This whole area had been given over to abandonment and enjoyment and the domes linked together here resounded to the hubbub. All this was being paid for by Terifia, in honour of the coming of age of her son, the Bolan, and in the eyes of the revellers she could do no wrong.

After this night, Hook knew, the title and the petty authority would pass to Bunji Cater, the trappings of a ludicrous nobility that still held the power, in this galaxy and in this day and age, of commanding respect and obedience from others. But the wealth, the riches, the basic sources of strength, would remain still with Terifia. She was a nice woman, full of her own power, with short fat legs; but she tried to do good in her own imperious way. She was not the kind of woman Ryder Hook would in the normal way have bothered over for a single second.

A group of near-naked girls ran past, clad only in strings of jewels and tufts of feathers, shrieking with their own laughter, their rosy bodies agleam in the lights. Two of Terifia's bodyguards watched the girls, their eyes like weasels. Hook watched the grotesque.

He saw the tensing of muscles in the old familiar way and he took a step forward, grasped the grotesque's right forearm and, with a merciless gouging of his fingers, bent the arm up and back.

The grotesque screamed.

All that pressure could not stop the neurologically-activated and muscle-powered dis-gel gun from jumping into the grotesque's hand. But he could not fire. They stood for a heartbeat, and then Hook clipped the arm further back so that it snapped, a dry tickling sound in the riot all about.

A bodyguard next to Terifia moved.

Hook knew what he was going to do.

He swung the grotesque off the ground, holding him like a club, put his feet into the bodyguard's guts. He let the swing carry him on, and yelled with a fury made more vicious at the brainlessness of Terifia's bodyguards.

"You stupid gonils! If you kill him now you'll never know who sent him!"

The bodyguard collapsed, retching. He would have shot and killed the grotesque and Hook both, and cared not one whit for either of them.

"Stay, Anton!" said Terifia.

She was not afraid.

She came up to Hook and reaching out a hand ripped away the grotesque's black diamond-dusted mask.

A flat and evilly-wedge-shaped head was revealed in which the reptilian eyes blazed with an emerald fire of hate.

Cast marks etched in acid across the scaled jaws showed the Trocoin to be a member of an honourable cast among that race of violent and vengeful people. He was a man who might be hired to kill other people. He was not in the accepted sense of the word an assassin; but the differences were shaded in tones of morality that meant nothing when the corpse lay charred and bleeding at his feet.

Hook cuffed him across those scaled jaws, and the screaming stopped. The swirling scarlet tails of the Trocoin's costume shivered and fell around his ankles. His arm remained broken and angular in Hook's grip.

"Ask him, Hook."

Terifia breathed deeply now, her eyes large and round beneath the makeup. The enormity of it made itself felt in her mind as an insult. She spat the question at the Trocoin.

"Who sent you to kill me, you curd?"

Hook waited, and then, quietly, he said: "You may never know, Terifia. He's programmed himself onto a self-destruct. He couldn't have been too confident, the poor devil."

"You feel sympathy for him?" Her tone lacerated Hook.

"It's a living."

"You're a grotesque, yourself, Hook, by the Great Salvor!"

"So I've been told. Who would like to see you dead?"

Her laugh shrilled unpleasantly.

"Who? Why, my loving son Bunji!"

Hook felt the distaste, and felt the sorrow, and knew it to be true.

Hook let the dead body of the Trocoin slump to the metalloy decking. The man had suicided rather than reveal the identity of his employer. No pro-assassin caught would do that. Around them the party raved on. Colours and lights and wine and women, laughter and songs, all the good things of the galaxy men and women fought and killed for – all of them dead and black forever to this Trocoin reptile-man at Hook's feet.

"You saved my life, Hook. You –" Terifia swayed towards him.

With a sinuous movement Hook avoided her naked clutching arms and, bending, riffled through the dead Trocoin's clothes. As he had expected he found nothing. The reptile-man had worn clothes and carried a dis-gel gun. That was all. "There's an irony for you, Terifia," said Hook, straightening up and letting the dead man's left arm flop back. The wrist credit card had dulled and destructed in death; but there had been time for Hook to read F.I.F. "Maybe you can trace him through your econorg."

"I don't need to. This is the work of my darling Bunji – I know it! I know it!"

On Terifia's home planet the women ran affairs until their son's daughters could take over. The men merely paraded the outer pomp. Bunji Cater quite clearly felt that to be a state of affairs needing alteration, and his male liberation movement had begun with his own mother. Hook knew of the dread secrets these young men must share. He wanted none of it. He just wanted a drink and a way get himself off Stellopolis in one piece – and preferably with money metal.

CHAPTER SEVEN

HOOK'S star cutter brought back to star city languished in space, parked out of the way by the disposal chutes, tethered by an umbilical cord and neglected. He had got absolutely nowhere with the city bosses. Terifia, after a try she felt she owed Ryder Hook for what he had done, gave up, saying rather testily: "If you're as big a gaff as you seem, Hook, and don't have the nous to join up with an econorg, then you deserve all you're asking for."

Even GCC had refused to pay any reward, pointing out with a logic that Hook would like to have stuffed them with that the Stellopolis police had recovered the money, not Ryder Hook.

Fifty kilos of art micro-recordings brought a very great deal of cash indeed. No-one in his right mind would accept that in money metal. It would be credited to his account, and his econorg would smile on him. Hook's money had been paid to him as he had requested. If he no longer had it, that was his hard luck. GCC would give him no reward for any help he had afforded the police in recovering the loot from the bank raid. And the Stellopolis city bosses wouldn't repair his space cutter until he paid them for the work.

No-one was being kind to Hook, and in that he saw merely his usual fate.

Terifia was being kind; but she cloyed after a time, and Hook suspected she had no idea of where to draw the line between benevolence and sheer self-gratification.

He enjoyed her, for although she was not beautiful and had short fat legs, she knew what life was all about. Oh, yes, he enjoyed her, and pleasured himself; but that could take only a fraction of his mind off his worries.

The four bodyguards from Anselm had disappeared.

They had been replaced by a much-enhanced bodyguard, of beings from a number of different races and thus pooling a variety of aptitudes. Terifia was taking good care of herself from here on in. What had happened to the four from Anselm who had so signally failed, Hook did not know. If Terifia had had them killed, he would not be surprised. To the lady Terifia that would be merely a just execution.

The Bolan, Bunji Cater, had also vanished.

"Gone sneaking back to his cronies, I expect," said Terifia. "And to think of the love I gave that boy! This is how he repays me."

"He'll try again, Terifia, if this funny little men's lib carries on."

"Funny it may be, and little; but I'm not laughing and it seems damned big to me."

The star city orbited about the planet of Voyden and the city-days passed. Hook felt that he must make another raid. This time he'd plan with a little more thoroughness and hit a Stellopolis outlet. He heard that the city bosses would have recompensed GCC for their losses; recovering the stolen money had seen to that. Payment for the damage, as always minimal in a society with immense recuperation factors operating for it, was taken care of. In this galaxy of the hundred and first century you could raze a city and they'd be cutting the ribbons on the freeways into the new one before you could turn around.

Taking a good look around, Hook was interrupted in his planning by Terifia's announcement that she had been invited by a city boss, one Lars Cu-Foylty, to sample the supreme delight of Stellopolis. Hook had heard people talking of the Curlmen's much vaunted, highly private and reputedly altogether wonderful pastime. They called it the Exper game. Reserved for the top people, extraordinarily wealthy and powerful visitors, denied to the ordinary run of folk, Exper was something that no-one should miss if afforded the opportunity.

Lars Cu-Foylty who carried within himself a deep knowledge of his own importance, had been gracious enough to allow the lady Terifia to bring Ryder Hook to an Exper session. It was a great privilege and honour. Also, it would result in a sizeable chunk being lopped from Terifia's bank balance.

"Oh, yes, Terifia," said Hook, in answer to the lady's bubbling announcement. "I agree in principle that one should sample every experience once. But in practice I consider it a foolish notion."

"Question is, Hook, are you a fuddy-duddy spoil-sport?"

"If I am, I am." He wasn't going to be gracious about this. He knew what Shaeel, his hermaphrodite friend, had had to say on various cutting and unkind occasions about Hook's sticking in the mud prowess. "You can have your arm cut off, if you like that experience. They'll grow you a new one, I know; but that's an experience I'd as lief be without."

"I don't know," said Terifia as she primped and patted her hair. She was wearing a vividly electric-blue hairstyle with many curls and dependent lovelocks that brushed around her naked shoulders. Her skin glowed that glorious golden tan of the peoples the galaxy recognised as of Homo sapiens stock. "That might be something to know. How you'd react."

"I'd react badly. Bloody badly. I have a strong dislike to portions of my anatomy being forcibly separated from the rest of me."

Terifia giggled, swinging around on the low stool so the hand-maid robots had to duck and glide to avoid her legs. Her body was very nice, very voluptuous indeed. Maybe ... "You could," said Hook, and halfway through the sentence making it into a laugh and a giggle and something that was nothing to do with what he was saying, "you could have your legs cut off. Get a new pair. Might be useful."

Her breasts, firm enough through careful attention, threatened to start heaving. Hook would not have cared to have Terifia become agitated, not right now. But: "You will have your little joke, Hook. I'm not an Earthwoman. I like my legs. Earthgirls have long skinny sticks."

"Oh," said Hook.

"Anyway, I believe in sampling all there is to sample."

"Like testing out an experience of death?"

"If you like," said the lady Terifia, swinging back to her makeup again.

Hook knew far too much about Death.

"Count me out."

She turned her head to look at him and now she was angry.

"I took a great deal of trouble to get Lars to invite you, you great ugly lump, Hook! Are you telling me you're not coming to Exper?"

"Of course I'm coming!"

"Well, make up your mind. While you've been off out gawping at star city Lars has been most attentive."

Had Hook been the normal male jealous of the female with whom he was currently keeping company, as they said, and probably with designs of marriage to follow, he would have leaped quiveringly alert. This was a danger sign. But Terifia, kind as she was, had managed to do nothing for him in the way of having his star cutter repaired. She was nice – true. But he would never tie himself for very long to one girl.

Particularly one who thought short fat legs were beautiful.

"You'd better get dressed, Terifia. We don't want to keep Lars waiting."

"Oh, Hook!"

Terifia's handmaid robots dressed her with finicky care and a lavish expenditure of powdered glitter-gems pressure-sprayed over her breasts and stomach and reaching over the shoulders. Her dress clung to her as she moved, and swayed and billowed when she paused. A silvery sprite, she seemed, with her towering mass of electric blue hair and her retinas tattooed to match. jewellery festooned her arms and of itself served as a covering. As for her legs; Hook did not smile. She must have taken some notice of his remark, for the allure slits of her gown were magneclamped up, giving her enough freedom to walk on her crystal slippers. She'd be wearing a tiny evening-out ag-pak in the small of her back and no doubt would soar most of where she wanted to go.

Hook, for his part, had changed into classically severe purple-black tunic and trousers, which he wore over his boots, and with a single splash of scarlet in the lining of the half-length cloak. His equipment snugged around his waist – Ton-ota, belt-pouch, ag-pak, med-pak all the rest of the gear a civilised inhabitant of the galaxy must needs take with him on an evening's entertainment.

Lars Cu-Foylty met them in his reception chambers, smiling, walking forward with outstretched hand in the accepted sapiens greeting ritual. Terifia twittered, clearly impressed, despite her own feelings of self-importance.

"So this is the maniac who had his cutter stolen and who is not affiliated with any conglomerate," said Foylty. He shook hands. The Cu was a mere signification of his high-standing among the Curlmen.

"He is a maniac, Lars! I've told him and told him. One day he'll learn the truth.'

"Assuredly."

Foylty led them through to a room in semi-darkness where men and women and aliens talked quietly, sitting in loungers, drinking any of a multiplicity of drinks immediately available. One or two idiots, as Hook sourly said, were smoking, a detestable habit Earth had successfully exported to her old enemies centuries ago.

They took the loungers indicated to them, and Foylty hurriedly introduced them to the couple sitting nearby. The man, florid, sure of himself, with a facial that concealed perfectly his true age and gave him the appearance of a man of a mere fifty, was chewing stim-gum. Hook knew that stim-gum was chewed by other than workers; but it was unusual.

"Now we're all here," Foylty said, breaking the low-voiced conversations into quietness. "We may begin. I believe you will be pleased with what we have found for you." He signalled his com-robots and the lights died completely. In the silence Hook could hear the gentle susuration from the breathing of these people all around him. He had only heard of Exper. He had no real idea of what to expect.

A pearly light grew on the far wall – at least, Hook could have sworn the radiance grew radially from a central spot on the wall; but after a time it was in his eyes, in his head, and instead of sitting in the lounger looking at the pictured representation of the scene on the wall, he was actually there in the representation. He was an onlooker on a strange scene.

"By the Curl of Curls!" The voice was Foylty's, echoing from a long way away, and yet, Hook knew, right here in the room with him. "We have latched a prize Exper!"

But the voice drifted and was gone. Hook became fused with the group of aliens who stood looking at a crude wooden wagon whose wheel lay pinned beneath the axle, splintered and ruined. Evil bat-like figures flitted among the branches, and ruby eyes glared brilliantly upon the half dozen aliens clustered around the wagon. Two weary mammoth-like creatures stood patiently in the shafts, their heads hanging, the sweat dripping from their coats. On the wagon was piled a heaping mass of household and domestic paraphernalia. A chill wind blew. Night was not far off, and these people were stranded, and the night contained hideous dangers.

"Right?" came Foylty's voice, again, intruding. "Are we all fused?"

A pause and in that pause Hook felt the first stirrings of a new and sickening emotion coursing through him. He kept shuttling between the knowledge that he sat in a lounger in a comfortable room in star city, and the unmistakable fact that he stood beside a broken-down wagon and faced the oncoming night with terror in his breast.

"Right," came Foylty's whisper, for the last time. "Here we go."

Hook saw the wagon under his hands, felt the hard-grained roughness of the wood as he struggled to heave the thing up off the wheel. Not that that would do much good. The wheel was smashed and they had no spare. Something howled most hideously off in the forest. The girl beside him jumped in fright. Now Hook understood what that new and pungent emotion was that flowed through him and loosened his bowels.

Fear.

He was terrified.

He, Ryder Hook, was shaking with fright!

He turned as a man ran across, yelling. What he said Hook had no idea. The weird double-knowledge went on, so that Le understood these people were not Homo sapiens, with their sleek chestnut-coloured fur, their wide and brilliant eyes hooded in bone, their bushy tails, their mouths which curved upwards and which showed the lip indentations to house the sharp tusks jutting from the lower jaw. They were not attractive, these aliens, they repelled because they stank abominably, and their sleek fur matted and hung muddily-tangled around their knees and the flat pads that served as feet.

The double-knowledge that Hook experienced expanded.

At once he realised this was triple-knowledge, a tripartite dismemberment of his consciousness. For now, as well as knowing he sat in a lounger in star city, and tried with despairing fear to haul a broken-down wagon up off its wheel in a forest that spawned horror – he was that horror!

For a third sensory impression surged over him, not driving away the fear that alien felt but supporting it and acting alongside it, in concert. For Hook glared with feral ruby eyes from the trees of the forest, and licked hungry chops as he sized up the prey below.

They would make good eating. He could imagine sinking his claws and talons into their bodies, biting huge chunks out of them, spitting out the fur, sinking his nose and teeth into the hot intestines! Oh, yes, Hook was going to dine well this night – and Hook was going to scream in agony and terror as he was devoured.

"Oh, yes! Oh, yes!" Terifia was moaning from the lounger next to him. He could not see her; but he knew she was in orgasm, and so he knew, too, that she had totally succumbed to the dark powers of the Exper.

The evening's entertainment proceeded. From the forest the bat-shapes swooped down, claws and fangs extended and ripping. Hook sought bloodily for his kill, and Hook snatched up a scythe and desperately attempted to fend off the horrors swooping from the nighted forest.

Terror and blood and agony engulfed Hook's mind.

The underlying motives of life and death were made manifest and hideously transparent.

For he was not just one person struggling with the cart, and turning, screaming, to feel his throat ripped out. He was not just one of the bat-creatures swooping down from the trees and rending and slashing and lapping greedily at the spilled and steaming blood. He was all of these. He was all the alien furry creatures with their pitiful wagon and he was all the malignant bat-like creatures and their pitiless fangs.

Hook for the moment could not break the compulsion Exper laid on him.

He was aware only of this combined essence of fear and of death, and of voracious hunger and of death.

He both suffered and triumphed. He was destroyed and he destroyed. And he did these things in many bodies.

His body shuddered with the repeated shocks, and his brain jumped and reacted to blood and entrails, to claws and fangs, to death and destruction.

Presently, after a while, when Hook had died the requisite number of times, Hook could fly back to the trees of the forest, engorged, trailing a dangling string of intestines from his fangs as he flew.

For a time – for a time – there was silence and darkness and exhaustion.

Slowly, like pallid dawn creeping through a hungover luxer's lavatory window, the lights in the room came back on and Hook could stare around at his fellow Expers in their loungers.

Their expressions were those of – not exactly of Werkler cats who have dined well on Werkler mice – but of a vacancy of immediate sensation and repleteness centring on the mind rather than on the stomach. They looked mentally bloated.

Lars Cu-Foylty stood up, spreading his hands.

"I must apologise most profoundly to you all, and particularly to our guests. But sometimes these things go this way."

The man chewing stim-gum snorted at this, and said something unpleasant about pasty-faced weaklings, and no real blood, and he was damned-well taking a rain check on this one.

"Certainly, my dear Felton. As I say, our control does sometimes let us down like this. I'll have the techs check the Exper out first thing."

Hook wondered what they were talking about.

He was well aware – now! – what Exper was all about. He would have said these people had had their money's worth. But this creep Felton was complaining. The Exper hadn't been bloody enough for him. Either that, or there was more to this than Hook supposed. He knew, now, what the Exper was all about; he still couldn't say how far the Curlmen of Stellopolis had taken their vicarious experiences of terror and death.

No wonder Terifia had been so off-hand about her reaction to his suggestion that she ought to experience death as a sure way of proving the proverb wrong!

This was one of the things Exper could do; it could give a man or woman the surrogate impressions of dying. Hook hadn't liked it. Yes, it was obscene, indecent, amoral; he could understand the scientific reasons for Exper experimentation; this use of the device debauched a man's spirit.

Fear! Ryder Hook had shaken with fear, back there in the forest, struggling with the broken wagon wheel, cursing the fates that had brought him to this, feeling the cruel ripping talons tearing out his throat, spilling his intestines into the mud, shocked and destroyed by spine-freezing fear. Fear! There were men in the galaxy who fed on fear. They joyed in the dark forces latent in the human brain, relishing that infinitely painful drawing out of terror and loathing.

And the obverse was true. The joy and hunger in killing, in destroying, in ravaging the humble and weak. That was a concomitant of galactic life, seen at its most refined in the way the multi-system conglomerates blindly drove over all opposition to encompass their desires. Of what value to them a culture or a people if that culture did not return the profits for which the econorgs craved? The two dark forces of fear and destruction had paraded like bestial phantoms in Hook's mind, and he felt the uncleanness of himself as a consequence.

"Well, Hook? Isn't Exper all they said it was?"

Hook lifted his chin at Felton, who was booming away in his complaining voice to Foylty. He, it was clear, felt he had been cheated of some very powerful experience.

"He don't think so, Terifia." Hook looked at her and kept

the puzzlement out of his face. "You really enjoyed that?"

"You were the one talking about enjoying every experience possible. Now you've experienced death –"

About to say that the experience was no novelty, Hook silenced himself. This woman could understand nothing of the linkages as between operative and control and second operative over the flashing non-telepathic links criss-crossing the galaxy. She wouldn't understand.

"And you're a better woman for that?"

"You are stuffy tonight, Hook! The Curlmen did us a favour. It costs to Exper, you know."

"I appreciate that, Terifia."

"Let's go, Hook."

"Yes. I think that would be – practical."

But he was not to escape thus lightly.

Lars Cu-Foylty approached, smiling, not arrogant with his power but exuding his consciousness of his position. Hook found a tiny trickle of amusement at the way Terifia automatically bristled up.

"I trust you enjoyed yourself, Taynor Hook. Although, as I have explained, the Voydun were not really co-operative. I am arranging a hunting party and would esteem it an honour if you would join us." As Terifia moved her shoulders, gleaming golden in the mellow glow, Foylty added smoothly: "You would care to accompany the lady Terifia, of course, Taynor Hook."

It was a statement.

"Oh, yes, Hook!" Terifia beamed happily at the Curlman, and put a beringed hand to that electric hair. "That sounds like great fun!"

"Then have your robots kit you up and, dear lady, be here after occultation tomorrow. I can promise you a marvellous time."

The stim-gun chewing Felton said: "I'll hold you to that, Foylty. After tonight I'm hungry for some experience."

"You'll get it, Felton. That I promise you."

As he left with Terifia hanging onto his arm and smiling happily, Hook wondered why on star city he'd allowed himself to be thus talked into a corner. But one thing was sure.

Terifia and Foylty between them had agreed he should go a-hunting.

Maybe, Ryder Hook surmised with a burst of passion, just maybe he might liven up the hunt for them.

CHAPTER EIGHT

TERTIA wanted Hook to wear the new pair of boots she had her robots buy for him.

The three-dimensional cube appearance tv glimmered away all across the far wall. They'd been showing over the network some of the selected items purchased from Hook's fifty kilos and everyone agreed the material was of first quality. There was even some music from the pre-space age, long since forgotten and known only from records that mentioned it in passing, or as footnotes. There would be a lot more to be said about that cache of pre-space age music; right now Hook was arguing with Terifia about his boots.

He'd lost his boots before, of course, and was likely to do so again. But it was a damned inconvenient business having to have new ones made for him. He waved his left boot in the lady Terifia's face so that she backed a step.

"Look at it, Terifia! What's wrong with it? I like my boots –"

"But they're *worn*, Hook! Surely you can see that!"

She had no need to explain the reason for her statement. No-one in this galaxy wore old or worn out clothes when new ones were available. Only slaves and those unfortunates of a similar kind had to descend to that banality.

"They've lasted well. Look, love, your new boots are great, fine; but I'd prefer to wear my own on this safari."

Safari. That was what Lars Cu-Foylty called the coming trip to the planet around whose flanks they eternally orbited.

Terifia would not be placated until Hook upended her on a suspended bed and ripped off her flimsy negligee. She wore a new one every single night, as was customary for a lady of her position. He studiously ignored her short fat legs and concentrated on those parts of her female form he really could admire and soon she was gasping and moaning and clawing at him and completely forgot all about boots, old or new.

"You're a devil, Hook! A black devil!"

"Yes."

"Give me some air – I'm suffocating."

"Finished already?" He nudged her flank and she laughed and they set to again. By the time he could crawl into his own bed Hook felt she wouldn't bother about boots. Mind you, he'd have to organise a pair of boots with a built in ag-pak in each one. He felt a distaste in the thought of sponging on Terifia for that. But a real pair of spring-heel-jacks would have been useful before now. He'd think about it ... He'd had a pair once; but they'd been burned off him and that had been that. Just before he slept he had an apocalyptic vision of the furry aliens with their unlovely features and brilliant bone-hooded eyes and flat clumsy feet and nauseous smell being ripped into bloody shreds by the bat-shaped monsters.

Hell and damnation!

The quicker he was off Stellopolis the better.

In the morning Terifia put up a tremendous fuss organising her outfit for the hunt.

She had the catalogues running through half a dozen different screens at the same time, picking and choosing, then discarding, until finally, with a pile to her waist of discarded garments she'd ordered and which had been made to her measurements and specifications, she kicked them all petulantly and flopped into a lounger.

"Nothing suits me, Hook!"

"Everything suits you, Terifia. Now, listen, you must have been hunting before –"

"Of course!"

"Well, wear something simple and easy and indestructible. Something to give you overall protection and fitted with a life-support system ... That's all there is to that. You should give this kind of concern to your weapons –"

"Go on, preach!"

"We don't even know what the hell it is we're hunting."

"Lars said to take a projectile weapon. He recommended a

Swan-Durk magnum for a waist gun. And –" Terifia put a hand to her forehead, pursing her lips, concentrating. "Now what did he say for the rifle? Oh, I don't know. Give him a call, love, and ask, will you?"

Hook found Foylty's com-robots patching the call through to the matra block. There was a slight delay and then the heavy authoritative face of the Curlman came on screen.

"Taynor Hook. I've been checking out the matra for our safari. You know the superstitions –" He lifted his left hand, negligently, and the sleeve fell back so that the credit card flashed in the illumination.

"Sure I know. They're not superstitions."

Foylty's heavy eyebrows drew down, a gesture with which he no doubt cowed his subordinates. "You are not – apprehensive, Taynor Hook?"

"Of course I am, Curlman Cu-Foylty." Hook felt it circumspect to address the man by a polite mode. "The transmat malfunctions-statistically-proven-one in a million times. I have no desire to be the millionth."

"Nor has anyone. I believe I can assure you that our matra here in Stellopolis will function well above the statistically-proven average. Is this why you called? I am rather busy –"

Hook kept his face its usual gargoyle of impassiveness.

"The lady Terifia wishes to be reminded of the rifle you recommended her to carry."

"Is that all?" The Curlman's reply spat too quickly, before he had time to think. Hook waited and Foylty caught himself. Naked power was never pleasant. "I recommended her a Krifarm Sharpshooter model four." Foylty turned his head to speak to a tech shadowed as a blur at the side of the matra fade-spot. "Fifteen point three two, you gonil! I'll have you castrated if you make a mistake!" He swung back to Hook, and he found a polite smile somewhere. "You know weapons?"

Hook decided that needling this Curlman would not pay a profit. "A little." He told a thumping great lie. "I'm no expert. But – a Krifarm, you said? In a Sharpshooter? Not a Zable-White?"

Foylty's expression would have curdled butter.

"I prefer a Krifarm Sharpshooter. The Zable-White has an electronic recoil reload system that I distrust. The Krifmans make a superior weapon with a magnetic action – as I am sure you know."

Sarcastic bastard, said Hook to himself. The curd clearly assumed Hook knew nothing.

"Very well, Curlman Cu-Foylty. I'll have the lady Terifia order herself a Krifarm."

"And you?" That came sharply.

"Oh," said Hook, and he remembered he was Ryder Hook, or at least, a little of what Ryder Hook was, in this damned star city. "I'll take the advice of my friend and stick with a Zable-White Sharpshooter model nine star."

"As you wish." Foylty was huffed over this, and Hook cut the connection and would have sniggered had that paid a dividend, too.

Terifia pranced about the apartment wearing a silver-glitter safety suit that clung to her most attractively. It had been sculpted to slide smoothly over breasts and hips and thighs, and the stretch under arms and between legs was ample and yet fashionable. Hook supposed he'd have to put up with a hunting companion who imagined the wild monsters, and the vermin and suchlike they were hunting, were going to study her critically as a fashion plate.

"Make sure, Terifia, you've got everything tucked in comfortably."

"Everything, Hook? Tucked in?"

Their relationship had progressed far enough for Hook to essay a laugh, and pass a country-remark that made Terifia giggle. She wasn't bad. Aware though he was that star city was working insidiously upon him and altering some of the values he associated with life in the galaxy, Hook felt in a hazy way secure in his own integrity, confident that he would remain Ryder Hook no matter what inducements were placed in his path. The slippery descent into the rich and comfortable life was all too damned easy.

The rifles came through the delivery chute, and Hook inspected them with the quick sure competence of the professional. He clicked the Krifarm up and handed it to Terifia.

"Don't blow your head off, love. You might find it useful."

She made the obvious retort as he checked out the Zable-White. Projectile weapons were always interesting in a culture where energy guns could vapourise metal and whiff the constituent atoms of people into nothingness. The linear magnetic field could whip the round out at high velocity, without the noise, confusion and recoil of explosive. The bullet itself was high grain, and of spitzer fashion, perfectly streamlined, for there was no need of a squared off base. The rounds provided came in solid and explosive varieties. Hook checked Terifia out as to the fit of her bandoleer. Some women had a natural difficulty in carrying bandoleers across their chests, Hook was thankful to know. The only forethought he gave to the damned safari was to have ordered the same calibre in the rifles.

When he put on his own safety suit of dark green Terifia cocked her head on one side and tut-tutted and said: "That's dangerous, Hook. You should wear orange, or a glitter suit like mine."

"So they tell me."

He clamped up the suit and made sure he felt comfortable. An ag-pak snugged in the small of his back. He discarded the notion of taking an anti-grav waistcoat. It was unlikely the safari would travel far from the matra block on Voyden. The med-pak was standard. He kept his Tonota-Eighty. In a society where guns might be worn, or not, Hook had been forced into the dismal position of feeling naked without a gun. That was a comment on the particular society in which he moved. Had he been a robot-clerk supervisor, say, or a tech, unexcitingly living out his life on a safe planet, he might never even see a gun from birth to death. But Ryder Hook did not live on a nice safe civilised planet. He spent his hectic life out on the frontiers, between the stars, and even this lazy hedonistic life in star city hadn't changed that in him, however much it had sapped his willpower in other ways.

He'd told Terifia in terms that would brook no argument that he would repay her – and with interest, if necessary. Hook had no holy idea that women were innately superior to men; but, equally, he wouldn't stand beholden to man or woman. He knew he was too damned independent for his own good. But Terifia knew that she could stop stone cold dead any thoughts she might harbour that Hook was a kept man.

They ate a long leisurely meal and watched some more selected items from the fifty kilos of arts material Hook had brought in, then he upended her on the bed again and showed her that despite having short fat legs he liked everything else she had, more than somewhat, and then they took themselves off to Lars Cu-Foylty at the matra block.

Terifia did say, however – and making Hook more resentful over her having to say it rather than what she said – that had Bunji's father been half the man Hook was he might still be alive now. Hook let that pass.

"You insist on wearing that dangerous colour?" Foylty looked annoyed.

"I happen to like it." Hook spoke lazily. Hell, if the monkey wanted to start a fight now Hook was in the frame of mind where he wouldn't walk away. As soon as the safari had been finished he'd be off. Terifia was bringing two of her new bodyguards; Hook suspected she might need a little more muscle than that down on Voyden.

"Very well," said Foylty. "We will go in as a party, we will take four trips, eight a time." He smiled his dark and powerful smile on Terifia, the smile Hook surmised he kept when he was plotting a big deal. "I shall fade with you, Terifia."

"That will be nice, Lars."

The matra block housing the fade-spot had been built early on in the life of star city and was situated out on a perimeter hub, a separate section of the city free-wheeling away in orbit around the planet. Enormous masses of power were required; but transporting down to the surface via matra was quicker and far less fussy than spacing down in a shuttle. Mind you, Hook felt a touch of the twinges when he stood on the red-painted fade-spot and the booth walls lowered around the party of eight. Breaking down a human being's atoms and shooting them through space and re-assembling them was a routine enough operation in this day and age; thought of that statistical probability that one in a million fades would result in error could bring out the goose-pimples.

"All set?" They all nodded like robots. Foylty gave the order, there followed a brief surge of power, the sensation of being kicked up the backside – but gently – and a vague disorientation. Then they were standing on the fade-spot on the surface of the planet Voyden.

Hook looked up.

They'd landed in daylight and in a wooded space floored with closely-growing ferns and there was absolutely no sign of Stellopolis circling high over their heads.

Terifia said, in a voice a quarter-octave too sharp: "We're all here."

Hook hadn't bothered to check. If the millionth chance had struck this time out, it hadn't struck him.

"This way."

Foylty led off, walking with a swing, his orange safety suit glowing under the sun of Purlon Major. The others followed. Almost immediately Terifia swore, and unclamped her kit and began pasting ointment on her skin. There were three other women in the party and they, too, began anointing themselves. Hook had slapped a fly off his forehead; strange how, although a spaceman, he didn't bother about physical discomfort that he understood was very real. They walked on towards the trees and the other three parties of eight faded down through the matra and followed them.

The day promised nice sunshine, no rain, and whatever sport the planet of Voyden could produce.

Terifia's two bodyguards walked alertly over the undulating carpet of low ferns, one in advance and to the left, the other in rear and to the right. Terifia, insisting that Hook walk at her side, walked on chattering away to Murl, the older and uglier of the two women she had told Hook she could put up with. The group squelched a little over the ferns. "Easier going on the edge of the forest," called Foylty. "But I wanted a clear sighting for the matra to transport us down."

Despite her chattering and the fact that one of her guards carried her rifle, Terifia at last swore roundly and said: "I'm not walking another step. I didn't bring an ag-pak for nothing."

Presently the whole group were flitting through the air ten

feet up over the ferns. Hook flew with them, although he had welcomed the exercise of the walk.

Hook liked trees. A single glance at the trees of this forest convinced him he could get to dislike anything given time. The trunks possessed that primitive scaly bark and greasy shining appearance that put him off any desire to touch them, and the leaves and branches jagged spiky and sharp against the sky. A few clouds moved slowly up there; what with the squelch below, the ferns and these disagreeable trees, only the good old sun could give Ryder Hook any comfort.

A flapping scarlet and green reptile form broke from the trees, a whiplike tail lashing, wide pinions beating strongly. Instantly, half a dozen rifles spat and the flying creature crumpled up in midair, falling like a smitten-moth, damaged and drab, tumbled into the trees. At that point Hook made up his mind to leave the safari. He had no need to run over once again all his cogent reasons in the arguments about taking life. He knew what he knew. He had absolutely no desire to travel across this planet shooting at the first thing that moved.

"I hit him clean!" shouted a fat man, waving his rifle in the air. "He's mine!"

"I hit him! He's mine!"

Two or three others joined in. And now Hook noticed a point that was in reality not worth comment. By chance all the members of the safari were humanoid in form, either Homo sapiens, or mal, or representatives of a human form very like that of Homo sapiens. It was only a chance; but it affected Ryder Hook.

The hunters speeded up and shot towards the forest, and in the lead flew those who claimed to have bagged the flying creature. Terifia looked at Hook, whose rifle was carried at the trail. "Give me my gun," she said to her guard. "I thought you'd be handy with a gun, Hook. You didn't even take aim before the others fired."

"True," said Ryder Hook. "I'm going back to Stellopolis."

"What!"

"You can cope without me here, Terifia. I'm not in the mood for slaughtering wild animals."

"You got a weak gut or something?"

"Probably."

"You great gaff, Hook!"

"This seems to be that gonil Foylty's idea of fun. It's not mine."

"Lars is a great hunter! He's often down here shooting."

There was no reply Hook cared to make to that.

From the sybaritic lifestyle of Stellopolis and the scientifically-controlled luxury and safety of star city, a jaunt down here must appeal to star city's inhabitants. From metalloy and plastic confining them around in shells of air, to this free-sweeping breeze, the sky high and blue above with the sun shining down in so mellow a contrast to the flaming ball of fire it seemed from space, the Curlmen must relish the deliberate descent to a primitive way of life. There were robots in attendance who had faded down afterwards and no doubt a grand picnic would be provided; but the idea of rustic simplicity, the great hunter stalking his prey in the evil wilds, the space and freedom of all this – oh, yes, Ryder Hook could well see why the Curlmen would go a-hunting.

"That flying reptile was vermin, Hook. Vermin!"

"Maybe it was. But too many people shot who couldn't know that. If that's going to be the way of it – no thank you."

Terifia's anger arose as much from her awareness that if Hook left it would be she who would look a fool in the eyes of these sophisticates of star city. Star City! Maybe Hook was right and they would do well to leave. As for her son, Bunji, he could go disintegrate himself for all she cared now he had come of age. He'd declared his intentions. So she knew what to do about them . . .

The main group had reached the trees and were poking about with homotropic and organotropic devices looking for the body of the kill. Other reptiles skeetered up in alarm, and the rifles began to pop in a regular succession, the linear acceleration motors hurling chunks of metalloy and explosive to rip reptilian wings and bodies into scaled wreckage.

"Hook! It's IQ. I'll come with you. We'll go to a little place I know, all sea and sand, gorgeous black sand that caresses you – oh, yes, Hook. I can't wait."

A thin whine scratched at the warm air. Hook glanced up.

One of the diamond-shaped skeeters used by star city to convey freight or people physically from planet to Stellopolis arrowed in over the horizon. Usually the Curlmen sent down a monstrous great freighter globe with a honeycomb of skeeter ports pocking the curve of the hull so that they might shift materials in bulk. The matra would be uneconomical here. Hook looked at the skeeter, at its narrow flanks and conical central bubble, one dorsal one ventral, and saw it veer in its flight and go slicing down out of sight beyond a clump of giant ferns. Someone was in a hurry.

"Did you hear me, Hook? Let's go!"

"Right, Terifia." He would be glad to get off Stellopolis; but he doubted if the black sand would be much more salubrious.

They turned and with the guards flanking them as before flew back to the fade-spot. The matra block here stood silent and in darkness.

"You'll have to call out, Prezwy," Terifia told one of her guards.

He said: "Yes, my lady," and reached for the call button.

His hand almost touched it. But there was no arm, no body, nothing attached to that hand, save a flare of supernal light. Hook reeled back in the heat blast. He grabbed Terifia. The other guard swung his energy gun in a panicky sweep that crisped fronds and ferns. Hook dived flat into the squelchy muck and Terifia yelped and then gagged as scummy mud choked into her mouth.

The second guard had left it too late. He vapourised in a second discharge. Hook flattened out, the Tonota in his hand, trying to see through the thick ferns around him. Another few seconds and they'd have been safely faded up to star city.

"Goddammittohell!" said Ryder Hook.

The anti-homotropic devices in his skull would keep off a very high quality device indeed, and no doubt whoever was shooting at him was fiddling with his instruments and cursing them for going on the blink at this minute.

"Oh, Hook!" quavered Terifia. She dribbled mud down her chin.

"Quiet, love."

"They're going to kill us."

"They don't know where we are, else they'd have vapourised the whole area around here." As he spoke a flash and a gout of steam and smoke broke twenty metres to his left. Another discharge ripped the sodden mud and ferns away farther off. "They're trying to find us. But they're going the wrong way."

"You know who this is, don't you? It's that mother-hating bastard son of mine!"

"Maybe."

Hook fancied it could be goons from Bandong who'd at last caught up with the creep who'd stolen a star cutter and fifty kilos of art micro-recordings. Whoever it was, they'd muffed their first and best chance, thanks to those circuits in his skull. But very soon they'd sweep this area, and by destroying everything in their way, destroy Terifia and Hook as well.

"Hook! Oh, Hook!" Terifia moaned with a kind of choked and sob-filled horror that had no place in Hook's scheme of operations.

"Keep absolutely quiet. They'll be listening out. I'll be back for you."

And Ryder Hook slid off into the ferns in a most ugly frame of mind indeed.

CHAPTER NINE

AROUND the other side of the silent silicon cube portal of the matra block the ferns grew more lushly. Hook moved between their sappy and bending stems as silently as the fade-spot waited to be operated. He went to throw the Zable-White rifle down; then paused, and finally slung it over his shoulders. You never knew in this man's galaxy what weapons you might need.

By keeping low he could maintain a profile that would not render him visible to optical sighting. If they had done what most people would have done and relied on a homotropic device, he should be all right. If they had radar it would be more tricky. He kept a lookout above in case they sent a spy-eye over to beam back a tv of him creeping through the ferns.

The sky remained clear apart from the clouds.

He wriggled on, and four more times heard the thumping discharge of a power gun and saw smoke and the dissolving cloud of disrupted atoms glowing into a miniature fireball over the ferns. It sounded and acted like a Krifarm model twenty. Potent stuff. He judged his moment and used the concussion of the next blast both to cross a small stream trickling soggily between the ferns and to carry out the last crosscheck on the position of the firer.

The person, whoever it might be, must be crouched down in the ferns, as Hook was, about twenty metres off to his right front. Hook put those famous old black boots of his down with scrupulous care. At his first blast he must do the job. If he missed, the Krifarm twenty would simply take earth and mud and water and ferns and Ryder Hook and whiff them into an atomised nothingness.

He crept forward, and halted, and slunk on again.

One more blast.

He daren't risk waiting for any more, for the circle was completing and the shooter was going to come perilously close to where Terifia crouched shocked and horrified on the muddy ground.

A clump of ferns before him afforded good shelter. He eased up behind them and carefully parted two stems and looked out. Directly ahead lay a wide and placid pool of water. It could only be centimetres deep; but it extended for a good ten metres. To cross that would be to expose himself. The next shot from up ahead would come close to him, and he daren't wait much longer. He slid the Tonota Eighty forward.

In that little silence with the sun glinting off the water in greens and browns, he heard a voice, low, rumbling, complaining. "You must have hit the sonofabitch by now, Art!"

"I ain't sure. This homotrop is plump crazy."

"She's enough money to buy an electronics lab. Get back to her!"

"That guy worries me –"

"Get the dame!"

Hook poised the Tonota carefully. He might not be in a Boosted state; but his hearing picked up words that normal hearing missed, and also he heard the suck and slither of the mud as the two men shifted uncomfortably. He aimed on the point of sound. One blast. If he missed they'd spray back at him and then – goodbye Ryder Hook.

He pressed the trigger carefully.

Ferns vanished, water boiled and whiffed away, mud gouted. Fumes and smoke blotted out the point of aim and Hook kept the discharge going for as long as he dared, well past the danger point. Then the auto cut-out clicked and the gun stopped firing. Anymore and it would have melted to slag in his fist. Give him a Martian Mega any time.

The wait was excruciating.

No return blast came in.

He let his breath out and stood up.

"Terifia! It's all right now."

She stood up and he was horrified at her nearness. The next one would have done for her. Only his homotropic befuddlement gear in his skull, presented to him courtesy of EAS, had saved their lives.

"You all right, Hook?"

"Yes."

She ran to him through the sloppy ooze. She didn't even think to use her ag-pak. She flung herself into his arms.

She gabbled at him, clutching him with arms and legs, holding onto him, screaming and shouting in his ear.

He had to get her back to reality at once – his kind of reality.

"Terifia! Where's your Krifarm Sharpshooter?"

She shuddered. She shook her head. "My – my what?"

"Your rifle, Terifia, your rifle!"

"I left it – I don't know! Who the hell cares about a lousy rifle! I was nearly killed! Don't you understand that?"

"Yes. Now we'll go back and find your rifle."

He took her elbow and guided her back, having to activate her ag-pak. The rifle lay half in a scummy pool and that annoyed Hook as much as anything.

"Fine way to treat a weapon," he grumbled. "Even if it is a Krifarm. The Krifarms make fine weaponry."

"Oh, Hook, can't you think of important things? There might be more of them! Bunji might have sent a lot – oh, Hook, I've got to get away!"

Hook wanted to find Lars Cu-Foylty. The great hunter had a problem he didn't yet know he had, and Hook wanted to hand it to him fast. He also did not want Terifia, in her present frame of mind, to find out for herself. He manipulated her away from the holocaust. One of the sprayed bursts of fire had vapourised the matra-block. The fade-spot had vanished. There was no way of return to star city via matter transmitter from that terminal.

"If he had sent more men, Terifia, we'd have known by now."

"I suppose so."

Many men might have gone into what they would regard as

a highly sympathetic job of psychological rehabilitation, trying to soothe Terifia, trying to relate general concepts of what they would regard as their rightful place in life with the dangers that besets all life. Educated people would know exactly what they were up to. Terifia would understand. For Hook these concepts were there to be studied but had no place in the suddenly violent environment in which they now found themselves. He knew the answers were imponderable enough to make him pragmatic enough to reach the end conclusions, and know there is no certainty in life. So he presented Terifia with those conclusions and acted on them, and cut out all the philosophic route in between. He often did this and wondered why people wanted to argue about matters that were clearly self-evident.

Probably that was why people he had known called him a tough bastard – and meant it.

They flew towards the forest where the reptile creatures were being hunted, and Hook took some comfort from the knowledge that Shaeel would understand. Ve could tolerate the rough tough barkiness of Ryder Hook, and laugh, and call him 'ook, and ve'd always come back as unreliably reliable as ever. This galaxy would be a goddammed miserable place without Shaeel around.

Lars Cu-Foylty and a number of the others who had not been completely absorbed in their hunting met Terifia and Hook halfway there. They were excited and apprehensive and yet quite without any real fear, and Hook's news had no real power to terrify them. Star-spanning civilisations gave to their citizens a power and a contempt for mundane matters. Rigging a new matra was a mere trifle. Cu-Foylty said: "I'll call Stellopolis after lunch. There is a party of Voydun in that forest somewhere and I want to roust them out."

Terifia had regained her poise. She reacted to the way Foylty took the occurrence in his stride, a mere trifle, annoying but of no importance. These Curlmen carried with them their surety of power quite beyond arrogance. They knew they controlled the powers of life and death and they had convinced themselves that they were most important people indeed.

Hook could not fail to be aware of this quality of assured confidence unmistakably displayed by the Curlmen; he was also tending to the sour belief that they thought too much of themselves by half; they were cocksure, self-preening, quite unable to understand anything not going the way they decided.

Felton excitedly chewing his stim gum so that his words gobbled out half-garbled yelled: "I've got 'em! The cunning bastards hid out in that arm of the wood – past that rock outcrop!"

A group of hunters winged up on their ag-paks, their rifles angular against the sky, eagerly searching.

"They're there all right! Come on! It's all IQ."

Terifia became caught up in the furore and Hook saw she was anxious to jump into this new experience in order to shut out painful memories of what had just happened. Everyone flew across the forest to the wood outskirts past a scraggly and wind-eroded jut of rocks. There were caves down there.

The Voydun had left their caves and hidden in this end of the woods. They had hoped to avoid the hunters. But they were tracked by homotropic devices that could sniff out a human being's betraying secrets and locate him unfailingly on a glowing screen. These Voydun were not equipped with any homotrop bafflement gear.

In company with the hunters but conscious that he had practically nothing in common with them, Ryder Hook flew over the jagged trees of the forest. The trees were those he had experienced nauseatingly in the Exper game; the same greasy scaled trunks, the sharply jagged leaves, the tainted colourations. People lived in that forest, with squelchy mud and ferns outside, and Hook felt sorry for them. The emotion astonished him a little, for since when had Ryder Hook had the great superiority in his own lifestyle to feel sorry for anyone else's? But, still, the Voydun lived in an unenviable situation.

"Now!" shouted Felton. He forged ahead.

Hook caught up with Terifia. The whole pack of hunters soared across the sky. The trees fled past below. Now they were out over the last straggling growths and here the encircling ferns had been razed a short time ago and had grown back in patches and only to knee-height.

The Voydun ran.

There were perhaps fifty of them, and they ran in crazy bounding leaps over the ferns, seeking to reach the taller growths beyond where they imagined they would be safe from these flying terrors of the skies.

Lars Cu-Foylty took out his pocket radio and spoke quickly, his mouth angled against the microphone.

"We have them now. Lock on. You'd better give three quarters amplification to begin with. Then boost to a hundred percent at the kill. Check?"

Whatever the answer was, Hook could not pick it up; but Foylty nodded in satisfaction.

Between the last few trees and the deeper growths of ferns lay this killing stretch of low greenery. A tech with Foylty looked up from the screen of his homotrop and said: "You won't need this any more." He shut the device down.

"Too true we won't!" screeched Felton. He lifted his rifle – it was a Krifarm Sharpshooter – and fired. The rifle made only that soft soughing sound of a linear acceleration job; but the explosive bullet sounded harsh and final, blowing off the arm of a running Voydun woman. She collapsed in the mud, screaming. A man halted to pick her up. A laughing woman from star city, poised on her ag-pak, shot the man in the back.

Other rifles coughed and the bullets tore into flesh and bone. Blood spilled to stain across the ferns and the mud.

A Voydun looked up, screaming, running madly in any direction from these dark hunters of the air.

"You getting all this?" Foylty was gabbling into his radio. He nodded, emphatically. "If you foul up you'll be castrated." More guns shot and more Voydun collapsed, bleeding.

Hook saw Terifia lift her rifle. He saw the blank, ghoulish, hungry look on her face. She was not beautiful; but she had been nice-looking and when she smiled she improved a thousand percent. But, now, in this hectic moment of blood and terror, her face showed bone-taut, scraped, burning with killing fury.

Hook took the Krifarm Sharpshooter away from her.

"What about that sea and that marvellous black sand?"

She turned drugged eyes to him.

"What the hell are you about, Hook? Give me my gun!"

Hook knew he was acting like an idiot. These Voydun were by nature prey. They lived down here on Voyden and the Curls from Stellopolis hunted them and exploited them and used them.

What difference was there at base between a multisystem conglomerate deciding a planet was no longer profitable and shutting down its enterprises there, and the Curlmen simply shooting these planetary inhabitants? In one case a planet would revert to a primitive living-style level, where probably many would starve before systems were redesigned. The econorgs wouldn't worry about that. They'd be taking their profits from another planet which for the moment was viable as a business locale. And in the other case the Curlmen were merely killing these people directly, with guns, instead of with the equally deadly weapons of interstellar economics.

The end results might be the same. But in Ryder Hook's eyes there were differences.

"This is not a game, Terifia. This is murder."

"Nonsense! Give that gun to me! By the Great Salvor, Hook! You'll be in trouble!"

"Since when have I been out of trouble?"

Felton was shooting away, picking his targets, gleeing. The others were shooting. Most were not very good shots, otherwise the whole group of running people below would have long-since been dead. Foylty took a shot at a woman and succeeded in blowing her head off, whereat he cursed and snapped the rifle up for a shot that would pay better dividends in the game he played.

Hook flew across and took the Krifarm away and threw it into the ferns.

Foylty looked at him as though he was mad.

Well – maybe he was.

He took out the Tonota and showed the muzzle to Foylty.

"You tell these people to stop shooting, Foylty, or I'll melt your guts down into slag."

Lars Cu-Foylty, the very important Curlman of Stellopolis, could not understand.

He tried to speak and Hook cuffed him around the cheek with his left hand.

"Shout, you bastard! Tell 'em to stop shooting. You've got to the count of three. One, two, th –"

"Stop!" screamed Foylty. "Stop shooting!"

They picked up his voice over their scarlet enjoyments. The shooting slackened and died. Felton, out in front, looked back. "You crazy, Foylty? I'm having fun!"

He shot down at a man and hit him in the leg. The explosive bullet tore the leg off high up the thigh.

Hook slid the Tonota away so fast Foylty didn't see it vanish. Hook's Zable-White lifted and, one-handed, he shot. Felton's leg vanished at the hip.

"Now stop shooting, you bastard gonil!"

The screams of sheer horror now came from a different source from the one from which they had racketted so recently.

"You'll –" gulped Foylty. He shook his head. "I don't know what you're trying to do. But you're a dead man!"

"Yes. Now shut up and do as you're told. Call out for a new matra. The hunt is over for the day." Foylty was clever enough not to argue. He called out over his radio and then Hook said: "And tell 'em to send down a medic team to look after these poor devils. They'll want whole blood as well as stellar plasma – and arm and leg buds for grafting. Tell 'em, Foylty, or I'll melt your backbone into ash."

Foylty relayed the message. He had to make himself unpleasant to his fellow Curlmen in star city before they understood the situation. The medical supplies and robot medics began to come down through the new matra block.

"Oh, Hook!" said Terifia. She floated near on her ag-pak, looking more disturbed even than she had immediately after the attack on her life. That she could place in context. "Hook! What are you interfering for?" She did not try to touch him. "I don't understand."

"Maybe I don't, either."

Hook knew with an unlovely self-morbidity that he'd been

talking a lot lately, talking too much, and not getting into any action. Well, this was more like old times.

"The Curlmen must organise the Exper, Hook! You know that. Why are you interfering like this, stopping them? They'll have to re-do all this tomorrow."

A chill of despair? Flowing icily through Ryder Hook?

Maybe.

He said: "I don't feel sorry for anyone in the whole damned galaxy, Terifia. I pity no-one. Justice comes to those who can pay. The more you pay the better the justice. I'm demanding payment now, with a gun; and these damned Curlmen are paying me – the payment is to get off the necks of these Voydun."

"That is quite out of the question," said Foylty. He had got over the impossible indignity of having a gun stuck in his guts by a madman. Now he was able to take charge of the situation once more. "The Exper has to go on. You have merely interrupted the programme. You are a nuisance, Hook, and will be dealt with back in Stellopolis."

"Hook!" said Terifia, and her face betrayed something more than Hook bargained for.

Hook said again that line he'd found interestingly useful before. He jammed the gun into Foylty's stomach.

"Tell me why I shouldn't kill you."

Lars Cu-Foylty gestured. His hand remained perfectly steady. He gestured negligently, in complete command.

"There are many reasons, Taynor Hook. You would die yourself, not necessarily immediately afterwards. If I am dead your protection is gone. You are a man who seems to object to killing, as witness your atavistic antics now, and whilst for the life of me I can't understand your stupidity, at least to kill me would be to deny what you seem set on doing. Are those enough reasons?"

"If I'm as stupid as you say I am, I don't need a reason to shoot your guts out past your backbone. Think of that."

Foylty flinched. But he came back with: "Hatred and violence against the Curlmen cannot move us."

You had to hand it to the curd; he knew what he was talking about.

The medics below were having some difficulty in sedating the wounded Voydun. The furred slobbery creatures would, with screams and shrieks, keep flailing away at the robots, trying to escape. But, after a time, they were all sedated and patched up, with instat-injects of blood, with plasma paks dripping into their veins, and those who had lost limbs having the buds of new growths grafted to the stumps. That left those who had had their heads blown off or their insides too badly mauled for surgery. Hook looked down and then back at Foylty.

"You murdered fifteen of them, Foylty. You and your hunters. The others have to be given a chance of life."

"You can't use that gun, Hook, and you can't keep awake for very many more revolutions of star city. I think we'll be back to carrying on with our perfectly proper Exper work soon."

"What you do with your faked melodramas for sick minds in Exper don't concern me. I just have this objection to your slaughtering these people for your amusement."

"You refer to the Exper you were privileged to attend?"

"Yes. Go back to the studio and shoot some more of those. You don't need real people –"

Foylty chuckled with a bright good humour that all Hook's gun had no power to quell.

"You are a fool, Hook! We have to do these programmes. What you experienced was not a dramatic representation. It was real. It was really happening. It didn't go as well as I'd hoped. What we have done here today, before you fouled us up, will give a great deal of pleasure in future Expers. We use real people, Hook, to give us our Exper fun!"

"You mean to fly there and tell me you kill so as to enjoy the feelings of death coupled in with killing – "

"I shot a man just now. When the Exper is through with processing I can relive this period and not only shoot the gonil, I can be in his mind and experience myself being shot. Believe me, Hook, there is no sweeter experience in all the galaxy."

Hook could see that.

He slashed the Tonota Eighty around Foylty's face, left

him drifting senseless on his ag-pak, and took off for the matra block.

The hunting rifles began to sigh after him at once, and a shell burst in a bright flash on the silicon portal. He left Terifia to find her own way back. He had an appointment with a star cutter – not his own damaged one but the first one he could liberate – and then it would be deep space for him.

Terifia's wail screamed after him.

"Hook! Wait for me!"

He turned in that weaving jinking erratic path over the jagged forest, shouted back. "Keep clear of me, Terifia! You're likely to get yourself killed!"

The new matra block had been set up in that cleared area of ferns, and his crazy flight for it circled over the forest and then bent inwards, like a boomerang. A medic robot trying to get out of the way was struck by a bullet and tumbled end over end, spraying wiring and transistors and blood paks and plastic boxes of bud-grafts. Hook ducked down beyond the mess. If anyone brought an energy gun into the play, now – it would no longer be play.

A thick half-drugged voice bellowed over the din.

"Don't kill him!" Hook recognised Felton's hate-filled voice. The man yelled more orders, waving his arms, for he was strapped to a para-med skeleton so as to keep the leg-bud nicely grafting. "Burn the matra! Hurry! Stop him getting away!"

Hook backpedalled furiously.

Despite Felton's ferocious orders the power-gun that crisped the matra block would have taken him into the blast as well. He felt the roar of displaced atoms coruscating about his ears. He was spun helplessly up into the air on the outskirts of the fireball, feeling the heat crisping the hairs on his body, scorching intolerably through his closed eyelids. The safety-suit gave him perhaps seventy percent protection.

At the top of the parabola he opened his eyes and looked down, everything tinged with luminous water-reflections of red and violet from his streaming eyes.

Like gathering barracuda, like closing jaws, like – oh, like any outriders of doom, the hunters closed in. The matra had been fused into slag. There was no way back to star city for Hook. The power gun in the grip of one of Felton's guards would vapourise him the split second Felton gave the order. They would shoot his arms and legs off first, no doubt, as a little fun, and no doubt couple that experience into the Exper so that they might appreciate it all again later, sitting comfortably in their loungers in star city.

If Terifia tried to intervene they'd do the same for her.

If anyone questioned the Curlmen the old hoary tale of a hunting accident would more than satisfy the Bolan, her son, Bunji Cater.

Hook stared down through streaming eyes at the scene, irradiated by violets and emeralds of sparkling prismatic colours, with the glittering crimson sparkling erratically at the sides of his vision. He shook his head. The smoke gusted in a little breeze, and he could smell the flat charred stink of burned ferns and greenery.

In the next second or so Ryder Hook would become just another expendable artifact for use in the Exper game.

CHAPTER TEN

Two ideas occurred to Ryder Hook.

The second was dependent on the first, and was to do with what he had planned for the futures of himself, the Curlmen and Stellopolis. That neat second idea had no value whatsoever, of course, if the first idea did not work. The first idea was to get himself extricated from this ludicrous situation. Ryder Hook did not like people shooting at him. The Tonota in his hand almost – almost spat a destructive blaze of fire – and then he eased off the trigger.

To slay these idiotic Curlmen now might be a justifiable process; it was not one Ryder Hook cared to follow.

Bullets cracked about him.

He cranked up the ag-pak to full power, put his head down, and dived headlong into the greasy crest of the smoke streaming from the fireball.

Smoke stung his eyes; but the eye-piece came down with a click. He ought to have done that earlier. He winged on in the cover of the smoke, and now bullets gave way to the cracking detonations of powerguns searching for him. He went furiously down the smoke column. Twice he almost broke through and the brightening light and thinning smoke warned him and he curved back. The brilliance of the energy-gun discharges smashed through the smoke, savage enough to illuminate his dark-green safety-suit and to make the polariser work overtime across his eyepiece. He hit the ground heavily, finding it hard and charred black, smooth as glass. He kept the ag-pak power full on and thrust with his feet and so, very much like a balanced free-diver, went careering over the ground until, with a pop, he burst from the smoke.

A single long dive took him into the nearest clump of ferns, brilliant and green and wet under the sun.

He didn't stop.

One thing about an energy-gun – if you didn't see your target before you fired you knew damn well you wouldn't see it afterwards. So that meant you wouldn't know if you'd hit. He'd experienced that one before, most latterly when he'd taken out those two clumsy would-be assassins. Now he worked his way through the ferns and over the squelchy ground. He daren't give the Curlmen a single sight of him. Once they suspected he hadn't been killed they'd be after him. He knew their own pride and arrogant power would not stop until they'd burned half the planet killing him.

Terifia was back there.

Any idea Hook might have harboured of turning and blasting the lot of them was ruptured by that single fact.

Hook knew he'd been growing spineless and weak and a great ninny in star city, and he couldn't blame Terifia for that. She knew what she wanted, and Hook knew what he wanted, and the two had not quite matched. But she'd been a good kid. Her son was out to kill her, and that made her much more interesting. Hook wormed his way through the ferns and he began to get back some of the special hallmarks that made being Ryder Hook so fascinating an existence in the galaxy.

"By Dirtie Bertie Bashti!" he said. "I do believe I'm enjoying myself!"

He was acting now – he told himself with some virtuousness – out of a sense not of injured amour-propre but of rightful justice. He'd damned-well give these Curlmen a rough ride! By God, yes!

The first Voydun he ran across cowered away in absolute mortal terror.

The ferns arched here seven feet over the slushy ground. The Voydun's sleek fur was sleek no longer, and hung matted and muddy and doleful. His great splay feet, flat as boards, were now revealed as being adapted to walk over the slush beneath the ferns. He carried a wooden spear with a fire-hardened tip. Hook mentally doffed his hat at this creature who had tamed fire and made it work for him in this sappy wilderness of water.

"Don't run!" Hook bawled after him. "I won't hurt you."

But the Voydun ran on without stopping. Hook could have caught him. But he let him go. He had an idea of what these people would do next – what he'd damned-well do himself had he been in their position – and so when, an hour later, he felt the fibrous net swing up from the quaggy ground and carry him up to swing three feet off the ground, wrapped like a cocoon, he did not immediately cut himself free. He lay there, swinging, and looked down as they crept out of the ferns.

There were ten Voydun, seven men and three women. They looked repulsive in a way Hook found repulsive to himself. Strange shapes in humanity meant nothing in this galaxy. But these people were shaped in such a way as, whilst not being untouchable, were pitiable; and that always made a man mad. Their tusks gleamed in the wet light. The sun was sinking and the fern-aisles darkened into a green twilight. One of the men prodded Hook with his wooden spear.

"I won't hurt you," said Hook. "I don't want to break your net, so loosen the thongs and we can talk."

The Voydun prodding him snarled. With those fangs the snarl was worth every pek. "No good talking to a starman. Only good starman is a dead starman."

Hook felt no surprise, merely confirmation.

He set himself to explain a few hometruths.

"If you don't cut me free I'll do it myself. Now, hurry up and make up your minds."

The spear point stuck in painfully and that decided Ryder Hook. He never appreciated physical discomfort.

He used the Tonota on low power and burned a few strands and so dropped himself down with a splodgy splash onto the ground.

The spears ringed him – didn't the idiots know the power of the weapon in his hand?

"I won't hurt you," he said, again. "Look –" He noticed the Tonota up a trifle and burned down a few dozen ferns. "There is what I can do – I won't do it to you."

He was talking to himself.

You had to be philosophic about this. What else could anyone expect? Here he'd come barging into their culture and telling them what was to their ears a pack of manifest lies, and then he'd burned the net and then flamed the sodden ferns – no wonder they'd run. In their place, he'd have run, too. Also, however, had he been one of them he'd have – yes – Hook ducked and swerved and the flung spear hissed past his neck.

That was to be expected, too . . .

"I mean you no harm!" Hook bellowed into the growing shadows.

He kept an eye open for more spears; but none came from the shrouding ferns.

A voice lifted.

"We do not believe you, starman. But we do not need to kill you. The beasts will do that in the night. You will die starman, and we will not have soiled our hands on you."

"I see you can recognise distinctions like that. I am not a starman."

He wasn't prepared to go into explanations to cover that. He was a man from the stars, yes; he was not a Curlman, and a Curlman was what the Voydun meant by a starman.

Somewhere in the dripping ferns a beast coughed, a giant chest-filled rumble that made Hook notch the Tonota up a trifle to a margin that would stun very quickly indeed. The charge would hold out for a good few blasts yet. After that he would have to see about a re-charge.

"We leave you to the beasts, starman."

Hook could hear them moving off quite clearly, and he recognised that they were moving with exquisite care and silence. No ordinary mortal would have heard them. Now if he was Boosted he could do the job in a hundredth of the time – and yet – and yet would being Boosted help him now? Ryder Hook had no wish to worry through the implications of that as he set out to follow the Voydun. All he knew was that he'd give a very great deal – a very great deal indeed – to be Boosted.

He had to win the confidence of these Voydun. He was

damned hungry. They'd have food. If he couldn't win their trust before his hunger got out of control he'd stand little chance of ever winning them over if he stole their food. He had to work carefully and quickly and keep a watchful eye out for the spear in the back.

Someway down the trail he heard the beast roar again.

This was no ruby-eyed bat-shape nor was it a reptile flier from the treetops. This was a predator adapted to hunting among the ferns. The Voydun went swiftly and silently along, and Hook followed circumspectly in their rear, his preternaturally sharp ears pricked.

By this time Stellopolis would have been circling the planet in its eternal orbit and be well on the way to another pass. Hook wasn't too worried over star city. There must be many thousands of possible routes for the city to take across the planet and they'd have arranged to come over this ferny section as often as necessary. From what Hook knew of the Exper game there were only a few areas on planet where the Voydun congregated, and all the chances were that they were not native to the planet but had been brought in as a suitable life form to inhabit this dreary place. The rest of Voydun would possess seas and deserts and ice caps and be capable of great beauty. The Curlmen needed an environment of basic unpleasantness to act as a catalyst in their equally unpleasant games.

The beast roared again. Hook caught an echoing roar.

Another night-time predator, up ahead, on the route of the Voydun, coughed menacingly. Hook hurried.

He moved with caution but he could not help making one silly big splash as he crossed a pool. A snag below the surface caught his foot. At once three spears flew to plunge with a hiss and a splash into the water. He went on fast, dropped to his hands and knees and crawled into a frondy cover. He peered ahead. The darkness now was only just above absolute, so that he could make out the forms of the Voydun as they shrank back on the pathway leading to a dimmer distance of shadows and ferns and trees. Something large and lethal coughed again on that alleyway between the ferns. Here the overhang had been sliced back and the stars shone down. They glittered in the sky – and they glittered in two spots of light fronting the alleyway through the ferns. The Voydun were trapped between monster ahead and monster in rear. They had allowed themselves to stay out too late in this terror-filled place because they had sought to capture a starman.

Hook shouted. "Keep your heads down, Voyduns!"

He slapped the Tonota back into the holster, slung the Zable-White off his shoulder and up. He took a single quick snap shot and pressed the trigger. The gun sighed.

The bullet sped true.

A violent splash of orange light lit all the sodden ferns and dependent greenery and blotted out the stars.

The beast howled.

Hook fired again.

The monster screeched and the third shot finished it.

Many a man would have stood up, elated that he had pulled it off. Ryder Hook swung about, hearing the deadly slither from the mud at the edge of the pool, and slammed four quick and raking shots into the greenly-black mass that rose onto six powerful hindlegs and reached a hungry snout and claws towards him. He fairly tore the thing's head off.

The huge body splashed backwards into the pool.

Then Voyduns were everywhere about him, carrying torches of twisted stems, dried against this use. The flaring lights spilled over the scene; over the bloodied water, over the crushed ferns, over the two dead monster bodies, and over Hook who slowly stood up, the Zable-White in his hand, staring at them all. He tried to smile. It was an effort; but he managed some kind of grimace they accepted.

"I told you I meant you no harm," Hook said. "And these beasties wanted you for their supper."

"You speak the truth, by the Sap of Life!" The Voydun who had been prodding Hook in the net nodded with great satisfaction. "You are a starman who is a fernman, may the Sap of Life fill you with joy."

"I'll take that the way you mean it. By Dear Old Dirtie Bertie Bashti! Look at this fellow's teeth!"

That monstrous alligator snout repelled. Hook could quite imagine an elegant Curlman in his lounger thrilling to the emotions of the monster as it chomped on a Voydun, and equally shuddering with a dread joy as he experienced the horror of being thus chewed up.

"You are welcome," said the spokesman. "We do not understand why you have come to visit the fernmen, but you are welcome."

"You've always lived here?" said Hook as they went with the torches flaring along the alleyway and so up into a rock outcrop in which deep caves provided dryness and shelter and warmth, for the night grew chill.

"Yes. Where else is there to live? We cannot pass the great waters, for we have tried."

Hook realised that this whole area had been walled off by sea and marsh and river. The Curlmen had themselves a planetary compound here, in which they ran the Voyduns for their pleasure. And if the star city had been in orbit around Voydun for two hundred years, that would be beyond the memory of the oldest of these people, for they had a shorter life span than interstellar man. Hook went into the caves, and marvelled at what he saw and the way the ferns dominated the culture, and ate red meat that tasted so rich he had to be careful, and drank water flavoured with a crushed berry, and began to talk to the Voydun, who called themselves fernmen.

After a time he found their abominable smell grow less repulsive. He had taken one sniff at the berry-flavoured water, and had thereafter figuratively held his nose as he drank. It tasted reasonable, quite refreshing after a time, and he supposed philosophically that the berry gave the Voydun their smell and that he'd be stinking like a cesspit also by now.

Over the other side of the rocks lay a ravine which carried water away into the ferns and bogs. Beyond that grew a kind of grass, against which the ferns had no chance in reproductive success despite the masses of spores lining the undersides of their fronds. Here extended land a little fitter for hunting and living; but the fernmen stayed on the limits of the ferny country, for this was an environment to which they had adapted, and two hundred years was microscopically small in the scale of evolution. If they stayed here for a good long evolutionary time they might develop running feet and venture onto the plains; as it was, their great splayed flat feet chained them to the swamps.

Evolutionary adaption served here as gaoler as well as physical boundaries.

The two great beasts of the fern swamps brought fresh meat to the Voydun. Hook could go to sleep on a bed of dried ferns secure in the knowledge that he had begun the outlines of his plan. It was not much to start with, a few scared flat-footed stinking fernmen and a bog; but it was a beginning.

On the morrow they demonstrated that they accepted him, and he set about setting a flame to the fuse that was going to blow star city out of the sky.

The beasts were cooked and some set aside for preservation. The task of collecting wood from the forest presented the fernmen with great dangers; Hook threw himself into giving as much help as he could. He knew the plan would take time; but just so long as the Boosted Men did not happen by, time was a commodity with which he was well-stocked.

The days passed.

He began to grow a grudging respect for the skills of these people; grudging because they were not Homo sapiens and smelled and had tusks and flat feet – and yet they were possessed of a primitive culture he had to recognise as being of value, a basic primordial culture far removed from the refinements of the cultures that flowered along the starlanes.

Contacts were maintained on a loose basis with other groups of fernmen in the swamps. The story came in some time later of a tribe that had been miraculously healed after a hunt by the accursed starman.

"May the Sap of Life run true, Hook," said old Fernmaster Torca, he who had prodded Hook in the net. "They are growing new arms and legs. It is something unheard of. I do not believe it."

"You can, Torca. It's true. But don't think the gonils from star city have gone soft. They hated having to do that."

On another day a mammoth-drawn cart came in with the news that a hut encampment had been burned and the Voydun burned along with their huts.

Hook noticed the way the fernmen greeted stories of the

horror surrounding them. There was no glee that some other tribe had been stricken, so that one might feel a little safer.

"When one suffers, Hook, we all suffer. The starmen hunt us with weapons of fire, like those you have. We do not know why they do this. They must have reasons we do not understand."

Hook had to work carefully. He did not want to get the fernmen to go off half-cocked. He contented himself with saying enough to begin the indoctrination process.

Soon there would be the summer solstice gathering when all the tribes congregated in the heart of the swamps. Here marriages would be contracted, different products would be bartered, those tribes famed for work in one particular art or craft exchanging their work for essential items they did not produce. There was even a rudimentary thing, a parliament; but it seemed to Hook merely a talk-session, and all the talk of the starmen and their latest atrocities. The Voydun married and bred and there were many children. The summer solstice gathering would see the genes of the tribes spread throughout the area they occupied.

"And do you not fight among yourselves?"

Hook had to explain what he meant, and even as he did so he wondered if he might not be a snake introducing evil into a garden which did not, at least, harbour that old evil.

Fernmaster Torca took it in his stride.

"We used to fight together. But now we fight the beasts and we reserve our energies to run from the starmen. If we fight each other we reduce our own strength."

Hook felt particularly delighted with that.

He no longer found the smell of the Voydun offensive, and the crushed-berry drink tasted palatable. He sore missed a drink of tea. But when he'd dealt with Stellopolis he'd drink tea until it came out of his ears.

They were chased a number of times, and hid in the ferns and in the mud and under the rocks. A few friends were killed. Hook did not shoot at the arrogantly flying Curlmen up there, firing down, relishing death and agony, and storing it all away in the memory banks of the Exper for their later degrading excitation. He remembered though, and, to his shame, Ryder Hook was a man who knew how to carry a grudge.

"Tell the other fernmasters," he said to Torca, as they trudged back to the caves, bearing the mutilated body of their friends killed in the last hunt. "At the summer meeting it will be necessary to talk long and to think exceedingly hard – and to plan. I wish to speak to the fernmasters assembled together . . . I want you all to assist me in doing away once and for all with the evil of the starmen."

He called the Curlmen starmen, did Ryder Hook, thinking now as a fernman.

"Are they not sent by the shrivelled Sap of Death to punish us for our sins, Hook?"

"*No!*"

Torca's ugly snouted face with the upturned tusks showed surprise and bafflement at Hook's vehemence. But Hook had been accepted as a fernman now. Torca said: "You are angry, Hook."

So where was this famous cool of Ryder Hook's?

"Yes, I am angry, Torca. There are evil reasons for what the starmen do to you. I know. I will tell you – but it is important that everyone of the fernmen know the truth at the summer solstice meeting. You are not being punished for some supposed sins." He went striding on in those old black boots of his, with an assist every now and then from the ag-pak which would discharge completely very soon. "You are a people singularly free of sin. You do not make war on one another, and that rates you pretty high in primitive – ah, that is, my friend, in cultures like yours." He'd almost blown it there. He was very wroth, was Ryder Hook. "You seek to assist each other. Against the starmen you have before had no means at all to resist –"

"But would not resistance itself be a sin?"

"My God!" said Ryder Hook. "Those bastards have you really brainwashed! I'll tell you –" Then he realised what he was doing, and simmered his anger until it came sufficiently off the boil for him to say in a calm tone: "Would not life be far more pleasant without the starmen's hunts, Torca?"

"That is an impossibility."

"But suppose."

"We-ell – yes, supposing. We could live our lives free from fear."

"Fear. That is the clue – yes, and the key."

They didn't have keys in the caves. But Torca took his meaning. There were slabs of rock on which records had been written down in long painful hours of scoring with stone styli; the fernmen had their own ideas of right and wrong. Their culture might be primitive; it had strengths the Curlmen could not suspect. Hook broke open one of the secret pouches in those old boots of his and handed the cavemaster's scribe a picklock of beryl-steel which would last a hundred years of stone-scoring. Everyone oohed and aahed as the scribe wrote down a record of the gift. Hook wondered what cultural taboo he'd broken now and what serf-slave-syndrome he might have set in operation. But it gave him pleasure to see the scribe writing away furiously without having to curse and fling away stone after stone that had broken or grown blunted. That pleasure was selfish, he knew that; but then – what pleasure in a gift was other than selfish, if you looked too hard at it?

One of the women came in crying on a day in which they had been out collecting fresh ferns to be dried on the sun-baked rock. Her son was dying, and no-one knew why. At once all the Voydun began congregating around the youth where he lay on a pallet at the mouth of the cave. They had a doctor who could cure wounds and stomach aches and use his ferny herbery; against the death reaching out for this young man he could do nothing. Hook noted how everyone shared the mother's grief. They felt a part of themselves slipping away with the decline of the youth. Hook diagnosed an internal injury. His med-pak was programmed to handle emergencies of a similar nature in the body of a Homo sapiens. Could the med-pak cure this Voydun?

"It is the shrivelled Sap of Death," said Torca. "The Sap of Life is over."

Tears streaked the faces of the Voydun clustered around. Every time death struck them they suffered all, every one, for the grief of the bereaved.

Hook unstrapped the med-pak and set it to what he figured would give the best chance. If these people had an appendix – maybe that would be it . . . He placed the med-pak over the youth's stomach and let the probes go to work. Medicines and chemicals were being pumped in, triggered by the analysis of the probes. Red blood – well, Hook knew the fernmen had red blood right enough. He'd seen plenty of it.

The people gathered were singing a long crooning sad song. The sun slipped beyond the ferntops and the torches were lit and pooling orange lights filled the caves with a radiance. Presently the youth moaned. Women had taken turns in bathing his forehead. Now his mother gave a shriek, and fell to her knees, and clasped the boy's hands in hers. He opened his eyes.

"Mother," he said. "Whatever is the matter?"

Everyone sent up a stupendous cheer of triumph.

The boy was saved. They took the Sap of Life as a symbol and the symbol and the sap had not deserted them. Hook was so far gone in their cultural beliefs that he didn't care if they were calling him a sap. He turned to Torca and everyone fell silent and listened as the fernmaster lifted a hand.

"We have been privileged to witness a great deed," said Fernmaster Torca. "Our friend Hook has destroyed the destroyer."

"You are all glad the boy lives," said Hook. "You grieved when death approached." He took a breath. When he spoke he made the words roll out, brave and full in the torchlight illuminating the caves.

"What would you think of a man or a woman who delighted in another's death? Who laughed with glee to see another person die in agony?"

"No! It is impossible! It is not one of us!" Their shouts racketted up.

The boy's mother, dazed with happiness, shouted over them all.

"I hate death with all my heart. To dream one could gloat over another dying – perhaps that one should be the one to die!"

"That is not worthy of you," said Torca.

"No." The woman lowered her head, her tusks gleaming in the torchlight. "No, I am ashamed. No one should seek death wantonly."

"Would you feel sorrow for such a one?" demanded Hook. "Would you feel contempt for him? Pity? Defilement?"

"Aye!" they shouted. "He would be a pitiable object, contemptible, and yet hardly worth contempt."

Yes, decided manipulator Ryder Hook, they were coming to the boil very nicely.

On the morrow a hunting party was out, for Fernmaster Torca's tribe would barter the flesh and scales of lizard-like monsters of the swamps for the more refined products of other tribes at the summer meet. The scales would be hardened off and the girls and young boys would puncture holes in them and thread them up into necklaces. The work was arduous; but everyone took their fair share, and Hook was in there helping.

Because they had to travel farther from the ferns around the caves they might be late returning. Each day of departure Torca would go through a long rigmarole designed to prophesy if a visit of the starmen might be expected.

"The devils will come when they wish, Torca."

"I would have said they came to punish us for our sins, for our waywardness, for not keeping to the path of friendship and help. We do not like them in a way difficult to explain, for we sought to slay you when we thought you were one of them. That was a sin, I see that now. But we had never before seen a starman alone in the ferns – we betrayed the Sap of Life –"

"You did what any man would do who didn't stop to think." Hook only then realised what Torca was trying to say. He had talked about not liking the starmen. Strange attitude to take, a man would say, to the beings who slaughtered friends, women and children. Now Hook realised, with a humility that angered him, that the fernmen did not hate. Hatred was not a part of their way of life. Dislike, fear – ah, yes, fear! They crept about in mortal fear of the Curlmen from star city.

The hunting party set off and Hook went with them. He still had a reasonable supply of ammunition for the Zable-White and he had not used the Tonota since showing off to his captors.

They trudged on, and Hook had to slog more and more as he didn't want to run the ag-pak right out.

Half a dozen of the hideous brightly-scaled bog-lizards were captured and put into the nets ready for transport. No carts would run here. The sun shone. They moved out into a pool and searched the surface for the tell-tale snouts. The lizards were almost as large as alligators, and twice as fierce. A cry went up, and the hunting group threw their nets. A wild thrashing in the water took all their attention.

Then – with a heart-stopping suddenness, a fernman screeched and twisted into the jaws of the lizard. The great jaws closed.

Hook glared up.

Over the tops of the nearest ferns a cloud of Curlmen on their ag-paks drifted, shining in the sun, firing down with rifles. The bullets scythed into the water, exploding in gouts of steam. The lizard was struck along with the man it had grasped. Torca gave a great yell.

"Run, my friends, *run*!"

Everyone set off splashing through the muddy water.

Bullets splashed and pinked all about them.

Absolute terror held the Voydun in a grip they could not break.

"For our sins!" screamed Torca.

Hook felt a blow across his back and stumbled forward. He was not wounded; a chunk of shoulder blade from a smashed Voydun had struck him.

He skidded in the muddy water, slipped, fell. A giant lizard opened its alligator jaws, bearing down on him. He saw the scarlet mouth, the yellow teeth, the gleam of black eyes in that squat scaled head.

The Curlmen above were enjoying their fun, shooting down on the defenceless Voydun below. Hook slipped and flopped in the ooze and the jagged jaws of the alligator-lizard crunched down on him.

CHAPTER ELEVEN

THESE ferocious jaws clenching down onto Ryder Hook's legs were equipped by a benificient nature with six-inch long fangs, hard curved yellow fangs that would puncture through Hook's flesh and blood despite all the half-boosted strengths of his body. And yet if he used the Zable-White in his fists now and blew the lizard's head off the Curlmen up there would know at once – at once for they would never overlook the obvious – that Hook was still alive. And then the powerguns would blaze in a cleansing fire and whiff all the pool and the ferns and the lizards and the fernmen – and Ryder Hook – into black oblivion.

Up to now they had not realised a Homo sapiens ran with the fernmen, and Hook wanted to keep it that way.

The fanged jaws crunched down on him.

He rammed the Zable-White vertically into those jaws muzzle uppermost. The butt plate spread the force and the massive closing snap halted; had he shoved the rifle in muzzle down it would probably have torn clean through the skin and membrane and flesh covering the wedge-shaped lower jaw. As it was, the lizard choked on the rifle and the jaws remained jammed open.

Hook dived flat half in and half across the water and made it to the bank where ferns closed above him.

Only an optical sight would catch him, for his skull-mounted anti-homotrop gear baffled the devices in the hands of the hunters' techs.

He glared up and the murder in his face mirrored and magnified that in the gloating faces of the Curlmen above.

"Stinking gonils!" he said, raving, cursing, his hand now

really shaking over the butt of the holstered Tonota. But he did not fire. If he shot all this hunting party there would be another one, and this time a fiercely-determined foray to obliterate him once and for all. And yet – and yet he did not cower in cover to save his own skin. It was not for his own safety that he refrained from shooting back.

Had he been alone he would have blasted the lot of them from star city, have battled them all from Stellopolis as they came for him.

Torca blundered splashing into the shallows and hauled himself up beneath the ferns.

"You have lost your weapon, Hook."

Torca appeared to Hook amazingly calm.

"Yes."

"They have killed enough of us now, and will fly away. We know their habits, and our sins have been paid for for a time."

The screams and shrieks faded as the fernmen reached their illusory safety, all unknowing that the ferns could never conceal them from a homotropic device. But the Curlmen were hauling off. Hook could hear them laughing and recounting some of the more splendid passages of the recent game. They were satisfied that they had instilled enough fear in the Voydun and had killed enough to provide a highly delectable session for the Exper. Continuous hunting was in their view necessary, for fresh people wished to experience both the thrill of killing and the horror of being killed at one and the same time.

Hook studied Torca. A little more research . . .

"You were filled with fear, in the pool, when the starmen were slaying our friends, Torca?"

Torca's brilliant bone-hooded eyes filled with pain.

"I was frightened, Hook, for is not that a part of the punishment we must endure?"

"It is not, as I have told you." Hook was as well aware as any galactic wanderer of the dangers of interfering with any culture, particularly a primitive culture. Taboos and beliefs were *there*; questioning them, interfering with them, could get you dead real quick. "You must have also felt that you did not like the starmen when they killed our friends?"

"That is true. I do not like the starmen."

Other fernmen splashed wearily out of the pool. The flying hunters whirled away, going back to the matra block and from thence to Stellopolis. They'd have a big party tonight, in the artificial day-and-night cycle of star city. A boy splashed up with his arm broken and held to his chest by the other. He was not crying; but his alien face twisted in pain.

"And is that all you feel about this murder affair, Torca? Just that you do not like the killers?"

"The Living Sap demands we live, and the Dying Sap demands we die –"

"But in your own time! Not because these curds come down and slaughter you!"

"It has always been so –"

Only for a couple of hundred years, Hook knew; but Torca would scarcely be expected to understand that he was a descendant of ancestors who had been brought to this dismal part of the world for sport and games. Doubtless the Curlmen had had other sporty planets to orbit before this. He read them as a people who loving luxury would always take the easy way out. Torca down here and his fernmen, hunted and slaughtered, took the road of fatalism.

"If I blew dried fern spores in your face, Torca, and you sneezed, you would not like that?"

"No. We use the dried spores and that would be a waste."

"But – would you dislike that more or less than seeing your friends killed?"

Torca shook his head. "I would not like either."

Hook felt a suspicion flowering in him. Why should not the Curlmen have implanted a command so that the fernmen and their children were incapable of hate? Hatred would hamper the enjoyment of the Curlmen. If he could get a good old scarlet hatred going he might rupture the Exper game.

The wounded were collected and carried back. The dead, also, were collected and brought in for the rituals demanded by the Sap of Death. Later the fernmen returned for the lizards. Hook got his Zable-White back. It was unharmed. He hefted the rifle and he looked up at the bright sky, and he pondered.

Even if by some trickery he convinced the Voyduns to hate the killers from space, that would not do what he wanted. He had at first thought that if the recording instruments could be swamped by concentrated doses of hatred, the fun and games would go out of the Exper. But he remembered Lars Cu-Foylty, as he remembered Inlander and Andrews and the other Curlmen of Stellopolis. They were accustomed to being hated, and their own self-sufficient pride would tell them how superior they were; hatred would not touch them. They were so smug, up there in their star city, lording it over these poor miserable creatures in the bogs below.

There were many other areas of Voydun that would be beautiful and marvellous places in which to live. Even the fernmen with their splayed flat feet could live more happily in a pleasant climate. They'd have to be near ferns, for a start, with the concomitant reassurance of the bogs and water; but gradually they'd move to more congenial surroundings, and they'd find forests that were not scarlet and jagged and repellent, and they'd build a culture of which any race could be proud.

All that was mere fanciful dreaming until the Curlmen of star city were off their backs.

So confident, so puffed with pride, so conscious of their superiority were the Curlmen. They'd treated Terifia and himself with that condescending patronising air that so infuriated a man. They knew they were envied in many parts of the galaxy for their luxury and their ways of life that gave them so much pleasure, and which they could sell to distinguished guests, providing them with the ecstatic spiritual convulsions of the Exper game. The inhabitants of star city were a supercilious disdainful bunch of bastards.

The humbleness of the Voydun infuriated Ryder Hook. He, the galactic adventurer to whom no man presented a problem, who cared not a single damn for a single soul – with the exception of Shaeel – found himself emotionally caught up with the patient fernmen and he hated every minute of it.

The situation had subtly changed for Ryder Hook and now he sweated out the days until the summer solstice gathering. At last the tribe set off deep into the heart of the bogs, and they carried out their primitive and pitiful attempts at covering their trail. A homotropic device would reck nothing of the careful wiping out of the marks of the tribe's passage.

The gathering convened on a boggy island in the centre of a massive area runneled with waterways and smothered with giant ferns. Enormous monsters cavorted in the pools, snorting and coughing with menace, and the way lay through dangers that brought the Zable-White into action more than once. But the tribes gathered. The boggy island contained at its heart a rocky outcrop, sheer-sided, steep, and at its centre a vast hollow worn from the weathered rock. Here, under cover of the ferns and of trees, the tribes met.

Hook took stock of all that went on, and, although fascinated by the bartering, by the dancing – huge ludicrous dancing on massive flat feet – and by the engagements that were made and troths that were plighted, by the contests of skills, by all the colourful activity, he fretted for the time when the speeches would be made and his time would have come.

"I have spoken to the other fernmasters, Hook. You are regarded with some amazement. Never before has a starman come among us."

"I hope you made it clear I am not a starman of the kind who fly above you and kill you."

"They accept that, Hook, for I have told them of what you have done."

Hook discovered that the fernmasters believed they would not be subjected to the divine wrath of the Sap of Death whilst they were gathered here. Never had they been attacked by the starmen when gathered in the great summer meeting. "There's always a first time," grunted Hook. But the chances of an attack on the gathered tribes was slender – and that made Hook annoyed. There'd never be a better opportunity for his plan to work. He had a plan. A weak, fearful, fragile little plan; but it was all he had. After the dispersal of the tribes, to make that plan work would be much harder than making it work now, with the tribes gathered under his intolerant eye.

Ryder Hook spoke to the assembled fernmen. Men, women, children, they clustered on the rocks amid the ferns, and all their brilliant bone-hooded eyes regarded him as he stood on the central rock with its carvings and hieroglyphs and lifted his arms and addressed them.

He began with a preamble in which he extolled the virtue of the fernmen. He told them a little of the galaxy and led them gently into an understanding that the little chips of icy fire they called the stars were suns, like Purlon Major, their own sun, and that many peoples lived on the worlds dancing around those suns. "There are men and women like you – like me – out there. I am just an ordinary man. The starmen are just ordinary men. They have not been sent by the Sap of Death to chastise you." He went on to drive into their skulls the facts he had observed, of their daily lives, of the help they gave one another, of their dislike of death and of those who caused death in other men.

He dealt gently with them, for they could not be expected to understand everything at once. But he kept hammering away.

The meet would last a full sixteen days.

In that time Hook by public oratory and by private discussion at least gave the Voydun a better understanding of their world, their place in that world, and the star city that floated so serenely by over their heads. There were many who did not believe; there were many who would not believe. Hook knew he was running out of time.

One comfort he had and a very real comfort it was, was that they would not burn him as a heretic. They listened. The Sap of Life could not command them to take another person's life. They were independent enough to want to listen and make up their own minds.

Their gentle approach to life when life impinged on other people made them give him a full and sympathetic hearing. It would be his fault if he failed. It was all up to Ryder Hook.

"When you slay a monster of the swamps, because it is going to kill and eat you or your women or your children, when you trap a lizard for its flesh and its scales, when you fish, do you gloat and glee over killing? Do you joy in the agony and pain you cause that which you kill?"

Shouts broke out at this from the multitudes clustered on

the fern-bright rocks. They shouted, shocked at the idea, contemptuous of any idea that Hook might think them joyful at slaying living life.

"Would you dislike a person who killed to give himself pleasure?"

They howled at this, and beat their flat feet against the rocks, and some danced up and down. They understood this well enough.

Torca spoke for them all.

"Such a person would be beneath contempt. He would be a null-thing, a nobody, less than the offal trodden into the slime."

"*Beneath contempt!*"

"*Aye!*" they roared back.

Hook left them shouting and arguing among themselves, for this kind of debate provided stronger drink than wine to their meetings. He had given up on creating hatred. He had thought to arouse their feelings of contempt for the starmen; but this reaction proved stronger than all. The fernmen felt a pity, a repudiation, a disdain, for the very idea.

Ryder Hook decided it was time he activated the final stages of this weak and fragile plan. There would never be a better chance than now. He felt a great and nauseous horror that many of his friends would be killed. But he could in all humility see no other way. And one clean final cauterisation would in the end prove more merciful than a long drawn-out campaign.

Ryder Hook made up his mind. He took his rifle and his energy gun and in his old safety-suit, now much bedraggled, he went off a-hunting on his own account.

His ag-pak provided enough power to fly him back to the area where he and Terifia had been attacked by Bunji's goons, and he found the diamond-shaped skeeter still neatly parked beyond the clump of giant ferns. The little craft opened to his loving ministrations with tools taken from his boot and he ducked inside. The twin cones of the central bubble housed a compact control cabin and a small area containing living quarters sufficient for the city-to-planet hops required. The big freighter-globes which carried the skeeters down on-planet would be filled with ore or whatever the Curlmen required from the planet and transport it up to star city. Hook checked the controls and then pre-flighted the section and switched on the various view screens.

Over the speakers a burst of local air-traffic came in, and he sorted that out with a spaceman's automatic shuffling of coded words, strings of figures, vectors, all the technical necessities of handling craft. He even raised a grimace that might have been a smile.

"Globe Ten to P.A. Nine. We are making planetfall."

"Check, Globe Ten. We have you."

Hook routed his sensors through to Globe Ten and then he chuckled. The Curlmen had sent a freighter globe down to pick up whatever it was this time out, and the globe was touching down less than ten kilometres away. There would be other globes out and he would have waited; the wait was curtailed.

The skeeter lifted and whined off towards freighter globe Ten.

The globular craft would not actually make contact with the planetary surface but would send out its fleet of skeeters from the ports pocking that smooth and curving hull. Very quickly Hook found himself flying over the hovering globe and could see the string of skeeters lacing away like beads.

The skeeter was equipped with a simple flamer up front, hardly a weapon, more an agricultural tool. Hook warmed the circuits and then triggered a burst directly at the massive globe hovering beneath him. His dive carried him on and past and he deliberately let them get a good look at him. He was taking an infernal chance, he was well aware of that.

The blast from the globe scorched all along the ventral cone of his skeeter.

The little craft swooped up in the air, flopped over onto her back, slid down. She hit the soggy ground with entirely too much momentum and the residual energy knocked Hook across the cramped cabin. The blow had little effect on his body; but he shook his head and cursed. They'd swatted him out of the sky too quickly.

He opened a channel and risked a further shot; over the

air he could hear them yelling about some maniac. He turned the gain up full and shouted: "You monkey's uncles are the maniacs! Tell Lars Cu-Foylty there's unfinished business down here! Tell him I'll shoot his guts out this time, for sure."

Hook burst open the canopy and clawed out. The little skimmer in its hatchway flipped up to his frantic stab at the emergency button. His own ag-pak was just about finished. He had to get away from the skeeter before they melted her down. The little skimmer soared away. It was merely a flat round plate something over two metres in diameter, with a shallowly rounded bottom. There were foot stirrups atop and Hook stood there, half crouched, dragging out the clumsy flare-gun from its bracket. The flare gun was designed as a last resort to give a position for rescue, if the skimmer radio was smashed.

The skimmer's anti-grav drive whined and Hook balanced easily within the field, his boots in the stirrups giving height, speed and directional control as he leaned in the desired directions.

He lifted the clumsy flare gun and let rip a string of bursts that soared out ahead. A thin pencil blast struck down past his right side, barely missing the skimmer, splashed coruscatingly off a rock half-buried in the mud. The rocks beyond lifting in gullies from the ferny bog concealed a hunter, then, and he was shooting with a Laranz-Pinner, there was no mistaking that intense and scorching beam.

The skimmer ducked down low and Hook crouched even lower, keeping his head down.

He had the skimmer going flat out, now.

At his back the freighter globe discharged a long string of skeeters. They peeled across the sky like an exploding pack of cards. Hook's skimmer went on over a ridge and then swooped down and the next pencil-thin beam from the Laranz-Pinner went wide.

That wild jolting ride finished with the skimmer hurtling beneath a frondy overhang of ferns.

Hook had created a bedlam out there. Foylty and others of the city bosses would be incensed. They'd come down to the planet to find out what was going on – and they'd guess Ryder Hook still lived. If that didn't smoke 'em out, nothing would.

There was no point in cutting into an apparat net. He knew with a sense of elation that came as an exhilarating drug that he *was* right. He *knew* what was going to happen . . .

By the time he got back to the meeting place he was in the frame of mind to have blown star city out of the sky, if he could have done so. As it was, he took a great and evil glee in the grief he was going to bring to the Curlmen. Or – the grief he trusted he would bring to them.

Now he had only to knock away the last strut and then the whole edifice of the Curlmen's hideous pastime would crumble.

He stood on the central rock with its hieroglyphs and he lifted his arms and the assembled fernmen fell silent.

"You have heard my words over the days of the meeting. You know something of the stars, and the peoples of the galaxy, and you know you are a proud race. I have told you that there are people in the galaxy who joy in the agony of others, who laugh at another person's death."

Their reaction was as before, but accentuated, for they had had time to digest and to think on what he had told them.

His ugly face chilled them as he went on.

"I grieve for you, for you are my friends. We are not made in the same shape. We are aliens to one another. But the starmen are made like me – and I am more alien to them than I am to you!"

There was much nodding of heads at this.

"You feel a scorn, a disdain, a contempt, for people who take life wantonly and joy in it, and regard it as a game. I tell you that the starmen do this! The starmen slay you for their sport, and laugh and glee in your agonies!"

The hubbub went on for a long time.

The Voydun could hardly believe that any intelligent being could behave thus. Their derision of that code of conduct rolled out.

"The starmen will be hunting you again, and soon, and here in the meeting place." He did not tell them why. That, he wished to spare them. "They will slay you and joy in it. You must not fear any more! You must not be afraid! What, how can a man be afraid of vermin who laugh as they kill him?" It was a specious argument; but what Hook wanted them to do hung on their refusal to feel fear. He need not have worried.

Torca said it for them all.

"How can a man fear such people? Death will come to us all in the end. We accept that ... They cannot be human beings, even if they are intelligent and can fly in the air and deal death with marvellous weapons. We scorn them, we despise them, we disdain them – and yet they are not worth contempt. They are beneath contempt. We pity them."

Hook looked at the multitude gathered, he saw their brilliant eyes beneath the bone ridges, he saw their fur, sleek now in honour of the meeting, their funny flat feet, their tails, and he felt a choking sensation that he knew had no part of the life style of Ryder Hook.

He checked the rounds left in the Zable-White's bandoleer, and he checked the Tonota Eighty, and he was ready when the Curlmen faded down through the matra and started to hunt Voydun.

The flying starmen swarmed over ... They shot down into the huddled masses of fernmen ... Ryder Hook found himself a nice little niche and he forced himself to sit there and not to shoot his weapons off and he made himself sit there and watch the slaughter. He saw Torca reel back with an arm blown off.

Torca lifted his alien head to the flying men above.

"You poor deluded souls!" shouted Torca, with the blood pouring from the arm stump. "Oh, how I pity you! You are beyond disdain, derided, outcast, *unhuman*!"

At last Hook could stand it no longer. He was inhuman himself most of the time; but this, he could no longer stomach.

He began with the rifle and he shot the damned Curlmen out of the air as he would have swatted flies.

The fires blazed back and forth, smoke roiled, and the fernmen screamed in agony when they were hit – for were they not human beings? But even though some of them broke down in fear and distress when a loved one was hit, their culture now that they saw the truth demanded their response could be nothing other than what it was. They could not hate. But their derision for the Curlmen pulsed in waves over the rocks and ferns.

Hook began using the Tonota and that decided the Curlmen whom, unable to spot him with their homotrops, at last broke off. They flew away. The shambles they left behind made Hook know he had no right still to be alive. But he was a rough tough spaceman, wasn't he? A barky galactic adventurer? So why did he feel like this?

Ryder Hook was out for number one. All the time. So why act like a maudlin sentimental fool?

The sun sank. The dead were prepared for burial, for what better place to bury the dear departed than in this place where the Saps of Death and Life so fatally intertwined?

The great summer solstice meeting was over. The tribes took their separate ways back to their homes.

Torca lived, with one arm. They went back to the caves.

Hook wondered and then rejected the thought. It would have been a temporary solution only to have shot the Curlmen out of the sky on their first attack. He could not stay down here on Voyden for ever. The Curlmen would have come back.

But he had no sure – no absolutely sure-fire absolute certainty – belief that what he had done would do what he wanted done. They went about the unending tasks of the fernmen's lives and they waited for the next attack. Hook withdrew into himself, and could not look at Torca without pain.

He had made up his mind.

He might have waited down there until he died of old age, or a monster of the swamps chomped him; he wouldn't leave until he was sure.

On a bright morning with the sun glinting off the water and casting a brilliance of green over the ferns he saw Terifia floating through the air towards him. She propelled a skimmer laden with supplies. She saw Hook as he waved and slanted down to him.

He managed a very nice smile for her.

"Oh, Hook! They said it was all your fault and I was to

blame and they cast me away down here! Hook, we're stranded!"

He helped her through the ferns.

"Tell me what happened, Terifia."

"You don't seem surprised to see me."

"I am! Oh, I am. Tell me."

"It was terrible! Poor Lars! We went to the latest Exper and it was a special one, for they'd made the recordings at a big gathering – something they hadn't done before. And – it was horrible, Hook, horrible!" She clung to him. The fern-people flapped out on their flat feet and stood in a ring, silently.

"Yes, Terifia?"

"The Curlmen – star city is such a wonderful place and they are so proud and masterful –"

"Yes. They are a supercilious bunch."

"But the Exper – we were made to feel like vermin, like little children – beyond contempt, even. We were derided! We were pitied! The star city – Oh, Hook – it was dreadful."

"It sounds highly enjoyable to me, Terifia. I'd like to have been there to hit that Foylty on the nose."

"It was far worse than that, Hook."

"Yes. I'm sure it was, I'm glad to say.

"And – Hook – Stellopolis!"

"What of star city, Terifia?"

"It's gone! The Curlmen couldn't stand the derision from the Exper. They knew the Voydun pitied them and they couldn't stand that. So they spaced out."

Hook lifted his arms and shouted to the assembled fernmen.

"Star city has gone! It has taken its evil back to the stars."

Torca, thin and drawn, spoke slowly.

"We understand – a little – of what you have done for us, Hook. But – will not some other planet suffer our fate at the hands of the starmen?"

"If that is to be, then the Sap of Death cannot be gainsaid. But maybe the memory of what they experienced here will affect them. Who can prophesy the fall of spores?"

Hook had once been highly conscious of the incongruity of his actions, given the relative racial characteristics of his present friends and the men of star city. He knew he had acted out of motives not primarily connected with his own safety or well-being – actions almost altruistic in their implications – and that worried him. He couldn't go on like this. He had to be out for number one, what with the Novamen searching for his guts to rip out. Some other planet would have to deal with the Curlmen of Stellopolis, and perhaps blow them all up in the process. That wouldn't bother Ryder Hook.

He could at least take a grain of comfort from the fact he had saved the Voydun. Now they could break out from these miserable bogs and ferns, find a good clean land in which to live, search for their own destiny on their own planet. Terifia looked about on the crowding fernpeople. "They look – strange, Hook. Uplifted. I'm sure star city was bad for them."

Hook looked at her. She still had Bunji to worry over. She thought they were stranded down here. Well, until he could find a net and make a surreptitious and totally safe call to Shaeel so that ve'd come spacing in to hoist him out, they were stranded. On Terifia's skimmer would be a tiny radio and he might jolly that along to call out to the stars. Either way there would be a little time to spend down here. He'd make damn sure he'd enjoy that with Terifia. Damned sure.

But first things first. He dragged out the skimmer's larger-scale med-pak and found an arm graft bud and so reassured Torca that he'd have a new arm growing back in no time.

"It is all very wonderful, Hook."

"Star city is off your backs. Now it's up to you. As for me, I've a little business with the lady."

He realised that Terifia had been wrinkling up her nose.

He knew why.

"Come on, love. Let's find ourselves a cave and set up house. We will soon be rescued, so we don't want to hang about."

"You're a plug-ugly, Hook, you really are." Terifia backed away. "And, Hook – you stink awful!"

"I know. Here, have a drink. You'll soon find the aroma irresistible."

Then Ryder Hook laughed. "You're better off down here with friends than you were on that Goddamned star city!"